Bring me back to you

Trena VanHoff

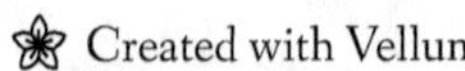 Created with Vellum

Dedication

To all the girls who dream of true love.
It's out there; I promise, promise.

Dear Reader

I will forever be grateful to you for taking a chance on me and my novel! All my dreams came true because you were willing to read my words. Never did I think I would make it this far, and I can't say thank you enough for your overwhelming support!

My first novel is also available on Amazon if you want to check out a dynamic story about a coven of witches, it is a Gilmore Girls meets Practical Magic book that is heavy on banter and loaded with fun. The best part is that the sisterhood they share is based on my cute family! Keeper of the Magic by Trena VanHoff. There is an insert of the preface and first chapter at the end of this novel to hopefully pique your interest!

Love,
Trena VanHoff

Check out my Instagram, Facebook and TikTok pages for book updates and behind-the-scenes information about the story and about being a self-published author! @trenavanhoffbooks

Check out my website for a way to subscribe for email updates about the next book I am publishing and for a little bit more information about the author: www.trenavanhoffbooks.com

Preface

It doesn't matter who you are; there will always be something about being near your best friend's brother that makes you feel like a teenager again.

Changing schools in high school was hard, but becoming friends with Caroline was easy. She was lighthearted in all of her actions. She was a friend to everyone and somehow managed to be the definition of sunshine. Caroline even looked the part with her bright blue eyes and blond hair that somehow always managed to shine. It was a massive contrast to the brown-on-brown combination that made up my features.

I was dull in comparison to her light.

We were sixteen when we met. Mom supported my desire to apply to the private school in town, and shockingly, I got into their scholarship program, mostly due to the school's low number of sophomore students for that year. On the third day of school, Caroline sat across from me at the empty cafeteria table and threw her hand across it in a way that showed she meant business, "I am Caroline Calloway. You are Felicity Abbott. We are going to be best friends."

She wasn't wrong. Twelve years later, she was still my best friend.

It was her wedding that we were celebrating throughout the next few months. Her fiancé, Richard, was traveling between D.C. and London for work, so we were throwing all the wedding parties while he was between projects.

Celebrating Caroline was easy; ignoring my heart pounding when near her older brother Wyatt would be hard.

Sixteen-year-old Felicity has been ecstatic to have a friend, especially one who didn't make fun of my often hand-me-down and faded uniform. I, however, was not ready for the influence of Wyatt Calloway on my heart, not that he gave me a second look back then.

My time with Wyatt Calloway started when Caroline convinced me to go out for the school's newspaper. She had been on it since the beginning of summer and argued that she could not do it alone. The school was short on writers; most students viewed work as an unnecessary stepping stone to their trust fund. Caroline liked that it kept her away from home, and she knew it would look good on our college applications, which was mainly why she pushed me to work on it with her.

Thankfully, I liked being on the paper. Having an excuse to attend school functions was fun, even when Caroline's brother Wyatt was forced to be our chauffeur. He hated it, but it made us feel special. Wyatt drove a jeep, missing the doors, playing into the bad boy persona that he pretended not to be aware of. Caroline and I would freak out that it would mess up our hair, but we were enthralled with being taken straight to where the hot seniors hung out every morning.

It was always a tight fit with all of his friends with us, but neither Caroline nor I were going to complain. We loved the attention it gave us. Not only did we have a crush on them, but we also learned a lot from the boys. Our rides to school were full of testosterone and often good advice.

It was Wyatt who told me to be a baker; well, suggested it. He was trying to quiet me as I had rattled about my upcoming class project. The project was one where we had to put down what we wanted to do with the rest of our lives, a challenging task for a teenager.

I was down to the last few hours before the assignment as we drove to school that morning. The drive was filled with Caroline and me chattering on, both of us trying to come up with anything to write down on my paper. It was easy for her; she had already decided on her plan as it had been decided for her long before she was ever born. She had her heart set on being a charity chairman, just like her mom and grandmother, which was just a step up from their previous position as debutants.

My Mom worked as a consultant at a bridal company, which was not a job I wanted to follow. There was no way I could become a chairman like Caroline, which left me wondering what I was supposed to do with the rest of my life. The boys gave suggestions, many of them pertaining to me wearing fewer clothes than I felt comfortable with, which I chose to ignore even if I was flattered. The only good suggestion came from the driver's seat. "What do you like to do?" Wyatt prompted my thoughts. "What would you do with it if you had an extra hour in your day? I read once that is what you should do with the rest of your life."

"I usually bake something." That was something that he typically made fun of me for. I always had a piece of candy in my hands or a container of treats to share with the people on campus once I got there, and he always told me that it took away from the image his jeep held. Betty Crocker and Bad Boy did not blend in his eyes.

"So do something with that. Become a baker and open your own bakery."

And that is what I did.

Chapter 1

Engagement Party

I stood at the side entrance of the large white Calloway home, directing the wait staff into the kitchen. I fussed over their white collars and black vests as they passed me. They were just arriving, which didn't give me much time to show them what they should be doing. I tried to make up for the time lost by shouting out directions. Caroline's dad, Steve, would not be happy to be paying for the time they were supposed to have been here, and he would not be satisfied if the party started before the servers got food on the floor. "Mr. Calloway is parsimonious, so doing your best is important if you want to be employed here again."

"Look at you, Flick, using fancy words. I'm impressed that you remembered any of them or that you are showing off your private school education. I thought you were still pretending you hadn't attended Riverside Prep with the rest of us." His presence made me breathless. His voice shook me in a way that brought me back to sixteen, watching the quarterback run across the field with a wink in my direction, primarily as he used that nickname, which I had always hated. Wyatt let out a long and low whistle as he took me in, his eyes taking note of the changes that had happened over the years as I went from girl to woman. Wyatt stopped when his eyes hit mine, and he gave me a deep look with so much underlining tension it was hard to breathe. "You've certainly grown up, haven't you?"

While it had only been a few days since I had last seen Caroline, it had been ten years since I had seen Wyatt Calloway. He had come to our high school graduation, and our families had been sitting together since they had become just as close as the two of us had, so it wasn't hard to find him. He hadn't given me a second look, staring at his phone for most of the ceremony, and chose to look up only when Caroline crossed the stage, even though I had tried to make eye contact with him multiple times.

While Caroline and I had stayed in touch, there was no reason to keep in touch with him, not that I didn't think of him often over those years.

"Wyatt. I didn't realize that you were going to be here." It was only three hours before the engagement party. This was the first of many parties I was in charge of as Caroline's maid of honor. I had the invitation list, and he hadn't RSVP'd that he would be here. Caroline said he would be in New York, and I trusted those words probably more than I should have.

He laughed casually, probably out of surprise at my dramatic outburst, "It is my parent's house. Am I not allowed to be here? I didn't realize our previous breakup had come with a custody arrangement."

House was a modest way to explain the building we were standing in and that he was raised in. His parents owned a large home that could only be classified as a mansion; it sat against a large lake with a beautiful white gazebo. There was no question as to why that was the venue for all of Caroline's wedding activities, mainly because it allowed her parents to brag as if their children's impressive college degrees were insufficient.

"You're allowed to be anywhere you want. A warning would have been nice." I had a mouthful of sass that I was unable to contain. I jutted out my hip and placed my hand on it to emphasize my point.

"If I remember correctly, you eat a lot. I'm not sure I ordered enough food, and you really should be watching your figure if you are going to be in all of these photos." I wasn't even sure why I said it or why I cared at all that he was here.

I saw the pictures from their family vacation and how good he looked in a swimsuit. He did not need to be worried about what he was putting into his body, and the Calloway's could afford to feed the entire state of Virginia without causing a dent in their pockets, so that wasn't a problem either. The kitchen overflowed with appetizers and multiple meal options for even the most restrictive diets. Most women who were going to be in attendance were so worried about losing their size two badge of honor that they wouldn't dare put a bite of food past their lips. I was just desperate to say something rude to him.

"Caroline told me you helped put this together. I remember your Mom always dreamed of owning her own wedding business. It's nice to see she made that happen." His face turned down to his phone while speaking; his thumbs raced across the screen. He didn't bother to look back up, not that he needed to remember what his eyes looked like. I remembered the soft blue they were and the way they almost turned to steel when he pinched his eyebrows together. "Hey, I've got to meet up with my dad. It was good to see you again."

Any words that I might have said froze in my mouth, so I gave him a pathetic wave as I stared at the broad lines of his back as he walked away. Thankfully, the staff needed my attention, so there was no way I could stay there looking after him, even if that was all I wanted to do.

I tried to shake off the weird energy my visit with Wyatt had left me with by returning to work. I hurried in to find the hired staff standing in the kitchen, where the house chef, Emsley, explained what would be served and how it needed to be presented throughout the meals. "This tray is caviar, and these need to be presented cold so it will be served on the metal trays with ice. If the tray feels warm in your hand, you need to return it to the kitchen so it can be put back in the fridge." She moved on to show another tray of the presented food. Emsley had worked for the Calloway family since we were teenagers, and she was an amazing chef. It was putting it lightly to say that she was a master of her craft. I was more than a little excited for the food options tonight. "This is shrimp scallops. They will need to be presented warm. If the tray starts to feel cold, then you will need to return it to the kitchen. We only want the best to be served to the guests tonight."

Emsley explained a few appetizers they would be handing out and then the meals before she directed them back to me. I tried to regain my composure and gave them all the smile I had practiced in the mirror. "Thank you all for joining us today. This is for the engagement of Caroline Calloway and Richard Chadwick. If you do well, Steve Calloway will keep the same team throughout the wedding celebrations." Although still frazzled from my interaction with Wyatt, I tried to sound confident. "And you want to do well. A good report from Mr. Calloway will set you up for many opportunities. Not to mention how generous he is when he feels someone has done their job well."

I saw all of them react, some in a positive way and some negative. I could already tell who would make it to the end of the wedding festivities and who wouldn't. Thankfully, there were more positive reactions than negative ones, which gave me hope we would make it through this without Mr. Calloway taking his often-lousy attitude out on me.

Emsley went back to talking to our staff, and I reviewed it enough times to memorize it. I let my eyes drift around the room while reviewing a checklist in my mind of everything I needed to do before the party tonight. From where I stood, I could see my mom, Lacey, walking through the ballroom, instructing a different staff member on where to put up the last decorations. She seemed completely in her element, and I felt pride as I watched her. The long layers of her brown hair were already done in tight curls for tonight's party, and her makeup was partially done with the plan to finish it off later. She had rushed through the getting ready process this morning since she was playing the part of guest and wedding planner tonight.

Wyatt wasn't wrong. This had been her dream for a long time; however, I was surprised he had remembered that. When the two of us were close, she was a bridal consultant for a large wedding chain but had always dreamed about opening her own wedding planning business. When she could finally open her shop, Caroline quickly signed on as her first bride. It was a stretch for her mother, MaryAnn, to hire anyone other than the best of the best. Thankfully, they had found a way to work well enough together that we had made it through much of the planning without many problems.

I left the staff with Emsley and walked through the large family room that had been stripped of furniture and turned into a ballroom for the night, just as it would be for all of the wedding activities. This is where there would be mingling before and after the dinner, primarily to present Steve Calloway with the opportunity to shmooze his associates.

The staff I had hired would handle the appetizers and drinks for all of the ballroom activities, while another set of staff was to serve the meal. MaryAnn was the one who made the executive decision to break the two teams up, having her regular party staff handle the meal since that was the most critical part and something she knew she needed control over.

"Honey, I'm glad you're in here. I was hoping to get your opinion on something." My mom drew her hand out towards the white curtains. They were floor-to-ceiling but usually pulled tight to block out the blinding sun. Now, she had them wide open so anyone standing in the ballroom could see the beautiful lake. "I have a team putting lanterns down the path to the pavilion and made sure there was plenty of light down there, just in case anyone wants to go by the lake. What do you think?"

"It's a little cold by the water. Do you anticipate people wanting to go outside?" Beside the water, there was always a sharp chill, especially this time of year as summer quickly transitioned to fall. We were lucky the humidity had dropped; I could only imagine what MaryAnn would have to say if every guest was slick with the layer of sweat the muggy air forced on the guests.

Mom shrugged in response to my question, looking through the window to the lake. She paused for a second to evaluate her work but then gave it a confident nod. She seemed pleased with her decision, which only made me feel better about my impute on the matter. "I suppose it doesn't matter. If they do, that's great; if they don't, then at least it's something people can look at. Not to mention a focal point." She reached out to perfect the curtain so that the panels lay flat. "It is also a way to have decor without overwhelming it."

She wasn't wrong; the view was breathtaking. Anyone could see that. I knew that a small part of me was biased since it was where Wyatt told me he loved me for the first time. The location will always have a tender place in my heart. He had done something similar with the space when we were teenagers.

He had strung over fifty rows of white Christmas lights through the railing; Wyatt knew they were one of my favorite parts of the holiday. He had also piled up blankets and pillows for us to lay on, using a large white sheet and a projector to display *The Princess Bride*, my favorite movie.

It was a precious moment that only the two of us shared. It was also one I hadn't shared with others, so I knew my mom wasn't pulling inspiration from that night. I thought about it most when decorating wedding cakes. It becomes easier to make happy cakes when you can draw inspiration from happy moments.

There were very few moments when Wyatt was authentic, especially when it came to impressing people. He was used to the typical pattern that his parents had set out for him: to use their money to get ahead. That moment out by the lake was a rare moment in time when he was just a teenage boy falling in love with a teenage girl.

I tried not to let the lines of past and present blur as the words tumbled out in a breathy whisper. "Mom, *Wyatt* is here."

* * *

Caroline paced the room in quick, short steps, and while that was concerning, it was not the sign of distress I was worried about. She was showing her nerves in the way she picked at her cuticles. Her fresh manicure looked a little worse for wear when she lowered her hands to her sides.

Her hair wasn't done, nor was her makeup since she had hired someone to do both, but her white jumpsuit was firmly pressed and ready to be put on. I could also tell she had already showered, and the maids had lathered her in a thick layer of floral lotion to preserve her fresh spray tan.

Her getting ready process was further along than I expected, sending through me a sense of relief. The last thing we needed was the bride to be behind schedule.

I let the beauty team in the door behind me. Three women came in and forced her into the chair before the vanity; they obviously had experience with brides like her as they, without words, managed to calm her down.

All three of them seemed to have a close relationship with a Botox injector by the way their faces appeared frozen in place. The redhead stepped forward, the only nonblonde from their trio, but she also seemed to be the pack's leader as she immediately went to work putting a round brush through Caroline's hair. At the same time, the other two unloaded their overflowing bags full of supplies onto the white counter before her.

It was no secret that Caroline was doing us a favor by hiring my mom's company for her wedding; the Calloway's could have afforded any wedding planner in the country and instead, put their money into the small business my mom had created. My mom was the wedding planner, and my bakery was providing all of the desserts for the wedding. Mom had been willing to go to the classifieds for a makeup artist, since that was not a skill either of us possessed. Caroline had her own team on speed dial from when she did her pageants, so that was no problem.

"How is it looking?" She wasn't usually classified as high-strung, but this was an important day, so all of us were willing to give it a pass. Her mother was passionate about this engagement party, which was the only reason Caroline agreed. If it were up to her, they would have eloped on a beach somewhere seconds after Richard proposed. Along with her heart of gold, there was the pressure to please people, which was why she was roped into having a four-part wedding. "Did everyone show up? How do they look?"

"Everything looks good. Everyone who needed to be here is here. Even some extras have arrived, *including* your brother." I could still see how the corners of his mouth rose with a smirk as he spoke. He hadn't changed in the years since we last saw each other, and neither had I. Somehow, I still felt like a fumbling teenager standing in his presence. "Thanks for the heads up; by the way, that was a *fun* surprise."

I knew I shouldn't be annoyed with the bride, but all rules change when you had over a decade of friendship.

She turned swiftly and barely missed hitting her head against the curling iron the women held. "He's *here*! He was supposed to be in New York this week." She was just as surprised as I was, which made me feel better. We never kept a secret from each other, and I was glad it wasn't starting today. "I can't imagine what he is doing here. He has a big presentation due tomorrow or the day after if you are going off the time difference."

"Well, he's not there anymore. He is downstairs in the office with your father." Wyatt worked for their father's business, Calloway Incorporated, which owned a multi-national oil company. He was preparing to take over as the CEO when Steve was willing to hand over the reins.

Wyatt had graduated from our high school and went straight to Harvard, where he got a degree in business management. There was no other path for him, even if he used to talk about what he would do if he were not set to take over his father's empire. His dreams of being a high school math teacher would have never been allowed, even if that was what he truly wanted. That was a long time ago when we shared secrets. I could only wonder what it was he wanted now.

"Oh my gosh, do we have enough food? We need to let Emsley know we have another guest." She asked the same silly question that had gone through my head when I first saw him. It was trivial for either one to question that, but as usual, our thoughts were in the same direction. "I know there was no way he told us he was coming. Is there a way we could get him a seat at the head table? Mom would not handle it well if he had to sit elsewhere."

I went over to the bar she had in the corner of her room and poured a glass of her favorite Chardonnay, then hurried to place it in her hand. It would help to calm her down. "Don't worry. There's plenty of food," I reassured her in a practiced, calm voice; it was one we had used on each other often. I poured myself a glass of wine and sat beside her because the drink would calm me, too. The free woman turned and started working on my hair while the other two worked on Caroline's. She quickly placed a detailed braid on both sides of my head. It was from the concept idea I had sent her, my hopes of keeping my hair out of my face tonight. "I haven't seen him in a long time. He looks good. I always knew leaving this town would do good things for him."

"I know you don't care, but he just broke up with his girlfriend. He told Mom it was because of their conflicting schedules, but I think it was not working for him anymore." She only gave this information because she knew I wanted to ask, but my pride wouldn't let me. Caroline knew I had never gotten over Wyatt Calloway, even if I tried to convince myself and others that I had. "He hates a relationship that requires work. She was hinting at wanting marriage, which he wasn't willing or wanting to work towards." Caroline wasn't kidding; that was the downfall of Wyatt and I, after all.

We dated in high school; he was eighteen, and I was sixteen. He broke up with me when he was ready to leave for Harvard. He didn't want to do a long-distance relationship, despite the fact that he would be coming back and forth to see his family. He planned to date around when he was at college and claimed that having a girlfriend was not what he wanted. It was better than cheating, so I had to give him that.

I hurried to send out a text message to my mom, asking her to find a seat for Wyatt at the head table beside Steve and MaryAnn. "You don't have to remind me of his inability to put in work in a relationship; that is not news to me." I got a confirmation text that we could give him a seat at the table and was quick to share the good news with Caroline since I had been the one to bring a grey cloud into the room. "He will be beside your mom at the head table, and my mom has moved Jenna to a table in the back."

A brother trumped a cousin, even one who was a bridesmaid, although MaryAnn would probably still have something to say about it. She was against many things I had decided on, even when I had Caroline's enthusiastic approval for the changes. This included the idea that everyone attending the engagement party also wore white. It was supposed to be a white-out party, a tradition from Princeton that Caroline was partial to when she attended. It was her way of breaking the stereotype that only the bride was special throughout the wedding planning, which drove MaryAnn crazy. She loved the idea of her daughter being the star of the show.

To appease her mother, Caroline planned that all the guests would wear all-black attire on the wedding day, forcing the eye to fall only on the happy couple.

The wedding colors were black, white, gold, and touches of greenery. It was a sophisticated way to blend the garden's foliage with the party. Although I had seen it on many Pinterest boards, she felt it was revolutionary. It wasn't something often done in her circle. They frequently went with a classic white and black with a bold signature color, usually red or purple, depending on the time of year.

I let one of the blonde women fuss with my makeup, touching up the work I had put into it earlier. I tried to keep my appearance on the simpler side, and I wasn't sure what they were going to want to do with me since two of them had eyeshadow up to their eyebrows, so I felt that I had made the right call. I knew that one of the Calloway's maids had already steamed my dress while another ensured my shoes and accessories were pulled out of my bag so they would be ready when I was.

Caroline went through her list, checking that everything was done or, at least, on its way to being done. She trusted me, but she was still a Type A personality with a fear of her mom. She paused on her list, then gasped, "Did the centerpieces come out okay? I know that my mom was against the gold vases. She thinks they are tacky, but I think they will make a statement."

And a statement they were making. It was in such a contrast against the black tablecloth, absolutely driving MaryAnn crazy, which gave me a thrill of satisfaction that I tried to ignore.

The three women rushed through the rest of our hair and makeup, leaving Caroline with beautiful Hollywood curls and a glimmer of silver sparkle covering her body, making her almost appear angelic. A series of maids helped her into her jumpsuit and tall heels. She had a long train hooked to the back of her pants, creating the allusion of a dress from behind.

"Care Bear, you look gorgeous." I tried to blink the tears away before they threatened to ruin my makeup. She did look fantastic, and by the look on her face, as she stared into the mirror, it seemed like she knew it. The women circled her a few more times to fix anything they considered to be an impurity. It was the same way vultures circled their prey.

I hurried to throw on my dress and said goodbye to her as I rushed out of the room. Guests would be arriving any moment, and it was my job as the maid of honor to play host until Caroline came downstairs.

The stairway down was beautiful. It didn't matter how many

times I had seen it; the grandness of each step would only continue to take my breath away. My hand gently sat on the rich wood of the banister; it was a gorgeous contrast to the beige marble beneath my feet. The Calloway's had custom-built their home, and MaryAnn designed every element. The grand staircase had always been one of her favorite parts and mine too.

My fingers lingered on the part that was a slightly different color than the rest from where they had needed to repair it eight years ago.

I could hear his steps before I saw him appear from the left side of the balcony, just as I had stepped out from the right. It felt premeditated, like he wanted to go down the stairs together.

I watched his eyes go up and down my figure for the second time today, only pausing when he found something particularly appealing. I took his distraction as my opportunity for the upper hand, knowing that I could not keep it long, "White looks good on you."

Wyatt laughed, and his hands flew to the ends of his cropped blond hair. It was the same nervous habit he had when we were teenagers, although I could tell he was desperate to mask it confidently. I could also see that he seemed to forget that he no longer had the long hair of his teenage years, as his hand appeared to fall short of where the strands used to lay. "And white *definitely* looks good on you."

He had a white shirt tucked into his pants. I noted that he had conveniently forgotten to button the top two buttons at the nape of his neck, was wearing a pair of khaki pants, and was obviously having thrown something together for the day. It showed how spur-of-the-moment this trip was for him, although it would have been easy for the Calloway's to have an outfit ready. MaryAnn probably already had one prepared on the off chance he did come. I could see him choosing not to wear it, opting for his own clothes instead out of spite.

His outfit would probably be a mess on anyone else, looking evident that it had been thrown together at the last moment. Still, it made him look so spontaneous and yet somehow dashingly handsome and carefree, which was something he was not.

The last time I had seen him look this dressed up was when he surprised me for my junior prom. We had been broken up for six painful months, and I was miserable.

Caroline begged me to go to prom with her, knowing that her date was planning to celebrate the night stereotypically, and she didn't want to end up alone. I was still nursing a broken heart, so there was no prospect of a date for me. Her parents' willingness to buy my ticket and a new dress sweetened the deal, although his surprise arrival threw me off.

It almost felt like a flashback, watching his body make the same movements it had done so many years before as the two of us stood in this exact spot. My body also remembered his movements as if they were my own.

"Are you ready for this thing?" His comment pulled me from my daze.

If he was going to be polite, then I could be too. I squared my shoulders and gave him that practiced smile. Around him, it didn't feel as forced as it did around everyone else I had used it on. It had been my main line of defense over the last few weeks, especially when dealing with his parents. "I'm excited for Caroline. This is everything she has ever wanted."

Caroline's entire dream was to live her mother's life, get a degree that she would barely use, marry a rich man (or at least one who had the potential to become a rich man), and then raise her daughter to repeat the cycle.

This was everything she ever wanted, and who was I to do anything but be supportive?

Wyatt and I stepped to the top of the stairs. He offered me his arm in the way his distinguished lifestyle had trained him for, "So what do you say? They are waiting for us after all."

I couldn't fight the laugh even if I wanted to. I loved how he could distract my attention from what I was terrified of. I didn't realize how easy it would be to fall back into our old pattern, especially after all this time. "I don't think we are what they are waiting for, but I am ready to face them if you are." I let his hand hold tightly onto me in a routine and practiced way that we were both so comfortable with, even if it had been a decade since we had been this close. "Just promise not to let me fall."

He leaned over to press a kiss to my temple like he had done a million times in our previous life. "The only time I would let you fall is if it was in love with me." He let his lips linger as he spoke the words. "I told you that once, years ago, and I think it's worth repeating now."

The shiver that rushed through my body had nothing to do with the nerves I had for the crowd and everything to do with the man beside me.

Once we got to the bottom of the stairs, there was already a thick crowd of people, which made me more nervous about my impending speech. It was only seconds before we were pulled in opposite directions. My mom dragged me to the kitchen since it was time to direct the staff while an older gentleman latched onto Wyatt; I could hear him state that he wanted to discuss an investment opportunity.

"They are ready to go. Team A has been split between food and drink waiters based on their age." Mom had a single wireless headphone in one ear that she was using to communicate with Emsley. "Felicity, you need to talk to team B. You need to tell them the line of your speech that you want them to bring out the champagne so everyone can be ready for the toast."

I had been tasked with giving a toast, something I was terrified of. Caroline didn't factor in my fear of public speaking when she asked me to be her maid of honor, and even though I was flattered, a part of me still questioned if the risk was worth the reward.

This impending speech was the very reason I had avoided food all day. I desperately tried to lower the possibility of throwing up on the guests.

Wyatt and Caroline knew better than anyone how nervous I got when people had their eyes trained on me for an extended period. As my best friend, it had been a self-appointed responsibility to take care of me after I made the foolish decision to join the debate team. I had been practicing taking a leap of faith; moving to their school was my first step in changing my life. I wanted to be braver, so choosing to do one new thing a day seemed like a good decision until that meant saying yes to the debate team, especially when I bowed to the social pressure from the school counselor who informed me how great it would look on my college applications.

Wyatt often cared for me since Caroline forced him to attend the debates with her. She was always so supportive, helping me plan and rehearse my speeches and then going as far as to attend all of them as well. I could always count on the Calloway siblings in the front row, just as I knew they would be as encouraging to me now as I spoke to the crowd.

I rejoined the party, trying to stay as small as possible as I followed behind a group of beautiful women. They were all following the directions from the butler at the door who had been tasked to direct the crowd into the ballroom, knowing that was where the future bride and groom would descend into the room, coming down the same grand staircase Wyatt and I had come down.

I anxiously pulled my cell phone from the conveniently hidden pocket in my dress. I had it memorized; I had read over it so many times, but I still carried the speech with me out of fear I would see the crowd and forget all the words.

I saw the Team B leader coming towards me, so I finished walking the gap to give her the directions. "When I tell them the power of their love is when drinks need to be put into hands." It was three lines before the end, and if I managed to read at a moderate pace, it would give them enough time. I chose that as their cue on purpose. It would require me to be aware of my speed since if they were not ready, I would have to stall, something I was desperate to avoid.

The teams were ready for their jobs, and I felt confident they would succeed without a problem. They all seemed competent and understood what was at stake, and yet I still hesitated to leave the team leader since that would mean the party was set to start.

I spun away from the woman, where I conveniently ran directly into Wyatt's hard body. I felt his hands come around my arms, catching me before I could fall to the floor.

"You still haven't figured out how to walk?" Wyatt's question would have potentially come off as an insult to an outsider, but I knew better than that, especially when it was paired with his signature smirk.

"Good thing you are there to catch me time after time." A wink came out swiftly from my eye, and I immediately regretted the decision. I knew I shouldn't be flirting with him. If I had let the anger from the past keep me back, I would have a better defense against his bright blue eyes.

He didn't see anything wrong with it, though; instead, he looked encouraged by this development. "Every time." He didn't let me go, pulled my body closer to his, and grinned somewhat like the big bad wolf. Wyatt took a deep breath, soaking in the smell of my body and perfume. "I will always catch you."

After a pregnant pause, he let me go, understanding that I had responsibilities outside his arms, but our closeness didn't leave me.

I wasn't sure if he was using this as his opportunity to ignite the romance we had between us so long ago or if he was finding this as his chance to flirt with someone familiar. There was always the chance that he was hoping for some casual fun now that he was back here and not in New York as planned.

There was too much for me to think about, so I brushed those thoughts aside, knowing that they were not essential and would only be something for me to fixate on later. If my mind were already going to overthink, it would only do me good to give it a purpose.

My body moved on autopilot as I walked throughout the room, greeting the guests in a way MaryAnn would be proud of. My mom's persistent work schedule meant that my house was often empty, so growing up I had at times been more of a sister than I had been a friend since I was at their house more often than I had been at my own. Steve and MaryAnn had even paid for me to go through the debutante program beside Caroline. Sometimes, I wondered if it was because they wanted me to have the same skills as their daughter. It was no secret that they valued her more the better she acted. They also possibly sent me through so that I didn't embarrass them when I joined their family at different social gatherings.

I felt the set alarm on my phone go off. It was letting me know that the happy couple would be coming into the room, and it was my job to ensure that the guests were all standing near the bottom of the stairs, ready to witness their arrival.

The band was prepared, so it didn't take long before I had a microphone in my hand. I took in a deep breath and tried to control the shaking of my nervous hands. "I would like to take this opportunity to thank you all for coming today. We are all grateful for your support and love for the happy couple." I saw out of the corner of my eye as MaryAnn gave me an approving smile. "Please, with me, welcome Caroline and Richard to their engagement celebration."

With my words, the happy couple began descending the stairs. Richard casually had Caroline's arm on his to guide her down the slick steps.

I announced that we would be going to the dining hall, and everyone followed behind the future bride and groom, letting them be their guide even if they knew the path on their own. As we returned to the dining room, the long hallway created a parade of people.

Team A brought the meals out, and they seemed to have it happen without any issues, at least none big enough that Mom or I heard about them. Emsley had taken them under her command, which was a great relief. If anyone were going to know what MaryAnn wanted, it would be her, the chef for all of the Calloway's meals and their elaborate parties that occurred year-round.

It wasn't long before the meal ended, and I returned to the front of the crowd with a microphone in my hand. I looked out at the group and felt comfort when I met Caroline's eyes, knowing that whatever I said, she would tell me it was terrific and be grateful that I did it.

My lungs filled with another deep breath, the shaking of my hands reminding me how close I was to the end of my speech. "There is nothing stronger than the love between these two lovely people. There is a power within your love that will keep your marriage strong; leaning into each other when one is struggling will show the amazing connection the two of you have. Even from the first day, I watched them together and knew there would be no one else for Caroline. She has been my partner in crime since we were teenagers, and now it is your turn to take care of our girl." I raised the champagne glass I had been handed and was grateful everyone in their chairs seemed to have their glass ready for the toast. Team A appeared to have accomplished their assignment, which made me feel better about how this wedding cheer would go. "I ask you to please raise your glass with me to celebrate the happy couple." I made the universal signal of raising my champagne, grateful that everyone followed as their mouths let out enthusiastic cheers before they all took a ceremonial sip.

I walked the microphone back to the band and let myself take a minute to wipe the thin layer of cold sweat, covering the back of my neck with the napkin I had hidden beside their drum kit. I took the entire flute of champagne in one enthusiastic gulp, grateful that nothing seemed to be coming up.

A hand laid on the middle of my back, startling me slightly. Wyatt had appeared without a sound. I watched him reach into the pocket of his khaki pants and bring out a brown paper bag. "No one can see you from this angle if you need to throw up." In the other hand, I could see a chill bottle of water that he must have smuggled in because MaryAnn would have never allowed it otherwise.

It was deja vu. He always had a water bottle and bag ready to go after those dreaded debate matches.

I dismissed the bag but did take the water. It went down

smoother than the champagne. "Thank you. I didn't think I was going to make it through."

"Make it through?" His face erupted in an enthusiastic grin that made his eyes sparkle. "Flick! It was amazing. You crushed it."

His positive attitude made me feel better about being in the spotlight. "You are right. I did crush it." I let myself fall into nostalgia, using the quote we had traded back and forth whenever the other did something we considered impressive. "Your vote of confidence is overwhelming."

"Breaking out *The Princess Bride* quote? You must be feeling okay." Wyatt's arms came around me as he pulled me against his chest. I tried to ignore the fluttering of my heart and the light kiss he placed against the top of my head.

Chapter 2

Junior Year

Wyatt Calloway was annoying.

He was beautiful in a way that didn't seem fair, considering he was a sixteen-year-old boy and already blessed enough to be richer than anyone I knew. His being annoying helped to counteract the beauty that was Wyatt.

Wyatt pulled up in front of my house and rapidly honked his horn despite the fact I was already walking down the driveway and that he could see me. He laid on the horn just to get a reaction out of me, and it always worked. Wyatt was driving me as a favor for Caroline. She liked that we could ride together every day, and I was without other options besides the school bus, so I was grateful for the ride. Anything beats having to ride the bus.

I had only known them for a few weeks, but our lives quickly became intertwined into a sibling connection. My life had previously lacked it, so I desperately soaked it all in.

I climbed into the backseat of the jeep, sitting beside Caroline and behind Wyatt. Sometimes, I wondered if it was strategic that it was my designated seat since it allowed him to make repetitive eye contact with me as he drove us the ten miles to school. He seemed to enjoy the opportunity to glare at me whenever our eyes met. I took advantage of my position in the car and stared him down while I spoke, "Wyatt. If only God had given you some patience, then maybe you would finally be attractive."

"If God gave me patience, it would have been too much for you to handle. You can barely handle being in the car now because I look this good." Wyatt winked back at me. This wasn't the first time he had taken our drive to school as an opportunity to flirt with me. It was something that I heavily encouraged, even if Caroline forced loud gags when she heard us talking. She told me she wanted to die at the idea of us going on a date. She was being dramatic; there was no way Wyatt would ask me out or ever see me in that way. He continued, breaking my thoughts. "I would become a god among men. You wouldn't stand a chance if I were perfect."

Wyatt was in the senior class, and driving to school with him gave Caroline and me a higher status than our junior position would allow for the hierarchy of the high school. His inability to stay away from me only raised my status, although he tried to brush it off, as if it was only out of convenience that he always found himself near me. Somehow, in the short time we had known each other, our souls had become magnets, and wherever one went, the other followed. I had a weakness in its powers.

This entire process had become so routine I could predict our morning's next steps without thinking about them. First, we pulled up to the school, where we would all exit the car. I would fix my ever-too-short plaid uniform, adjusting my bag on my shoulder. Caroline would wave to anyone watching as if she were a celebrity, and then she would hurry on to her first class; she had a crush on her chemistry partner, who was recently single. Secondly, Wyatt and I would make the slow, mundane walk to the hall of English and creative arts classes. Third, we would avoid how our hands brushed together as we walked.

We both knew that we didn't have to walk together and that it didn't make sense for us to do it since there were a hundred other people we could have walked with. The football players would want to spend time with Wyatt and the girls, dying to be at his side. Their envious looks helped me to stand taller.

"Did you finish the paper for Mrs. Wilk's class?" He casually hung his Prada backpack off his shoulder and held his textbooks on the other side of his body. He looked less like a student and more like a model in a back-to-school ad. He made our standard private school uniform look nicer than it was.

Wyatt and I were in the same honors English class. He had been annoyed when I entered the classroom on my first day. Realizing that his sister's friend had tested into senior-level English and that she would also be in his classes did not spark joy in him; that was obvious by the grimaced expression on his face. It got even worse when I was seated beside him, as the teacher chose to use alphabetical order for her seating chart. We often found this when we ended up in the same classes, which happened even more often as we tried to get through the extracurricular classes like ceramics and student government.

We conveniently sat beside each other or within arm's distance in every class, which drove him crazy, often referring to me as his shadow. He would tell his friends, "No matter what I do, my shadow is always there," as if I had a single say on the matter. It was a small school, and there were only so many places for one person to be. Wyatt had to admit our shared classes helped when the Calloway siblings and I sat at their dining room table to work on our homework, discussing the questions when needed and sharing material. It also helped us both to be better in our classes, wanting to compete against each other in a way Caroline considered silly.

Her love for school was much lower than Wyatt's and mine, although the love the two of us had for it was for different reasons. He was fighting to hold his own in a world where his father dominated while I was battling for a scholarship, which was how we ended up sitting across from each other with matching worn copies of *Pride and Prejudice* while she went off to the mall with our friends. She was in standard junior English, and they were reading *To Kill A Mockingbird*; the message behind that story was an understanding of human nature, what is good and what is inherently evil. She claimed to have grasped this after reading the SparkNotes version of the book and listening to the movie, having it play in the background while she played on her phone.

"This book is so boring. I don't know how you call this your favorite." He had flipped a single pen between his fingers as I read the chapter aloud but paused, fidgeting when he spoke like he couldn't do both things simultaneously. English wasn't his favorite for a few reasons, so his classifying it as boring wasn't new to me.

Although he loved school, he hated what school represented. It was just another thing for his dad to hang over his head, always stating how much easier his son had it or how much better he had been. Wyatt secretly had dyslexia, which didn't help instill a love for our English class either. He didn't want to share that with others, especially our peers, so we often studied alone in the secluded corners of their homes.

He hadn't needed to tell me about his condition; I had figured it out on my own. The signs were there if you knew what you were looking for, like how Wyatt always chose to listen to his textbooks when that was an option. He would voice text or just avoid texting by making a phone call. I mostly saw the signs of how his motions and actions emulated my mom and how she forced herself to adapt to the world that was not set up to help her.

Mom barely supported my going to Private School, even if that's what I fought so hard to get there. I think it was because she had hardened her heart against the elite long before I came around. While she saw them as stuck-up snobs, I saw them as my opportunity to step up in the world.

Our school loved to show that they were inclusive and willing to do anything to provide students with a proper education; at least, that was what the posters they had posted everywhere encouraged. That wasn't true when it came to learning conditions such as dyslexia. They didn't care to help students in classes by providing better resources when they needed them, not that he often asked for help.

"It's a balance of two people coming together and ignoring their differences." It was my favorite story. I had read it more times than I cared to admit, so I was probably the best person for him to study with. It also helped that I didn't have to learn the material as he did, and I was willing to go at the pace he needed since studying wasn't a priority. "That is a major reason why it's my favorite."

It also felt like it was the synopsis for my entire life now that I had become a regular in their glamorous lives. Knowing how it would set him off, I choose not to share that reason with Wyatt.

He held his book closer to his face as if that would help him and slowly read directly from the text. "When she is secure of him, there will be leisure for falling in love as much as she chooses." Wyatt dropped the book, and his face looked perplexed. "What is that supposed to mean? What does leisure have to do with love? I don't understand why they can't just say what they mean instead of saying a million words that force you to figure out what they are saying." He rolled his eyes, but there was a deeper frustration there. "How am I supposed to understand it if they intentionally confuse it?"

"Would it help to consider it slang? We might use the word rad to describe something crazy or something we admire when the rest of the world considers this a bad thing. By the time the next generation of kids are in school, using the word rad in that way will probably be considered stupid, and they will laugh at them for being out of style."

He only shook his head at me. His lips were curled into the faintest smirk he was failing to disguise. "Flick, no one has called something rad since the eighties. You are the one out of style." I could feel the blush of embarrassment rush to my cheeks. "I understand what you are saying, though."

Wyatt had recently started calling me Flick, which was initially annoying, especially since he had pretended not to know my name, acting as if he genuinely thought my name was Flick despite that being an adjective and not anything close to a real name. He used it in such an endearing way now that I could feel myself soften, even if it was only by a little.

I tried to pretend my face wasn't the same shade as the tomatoes in our lunch salads while I explained what he had just read. "This is a perfect part. Charlotte says this to Elizabeth, giving her opinion on Jane's effort to find a husband. Charlotte doesn't think love is important for Jane, and that she barely knows anything about him. While this is important to some people, not important to others." I rattled off my response quickly, but his face remained unchanged from the previous confusion, so I took another approach. "It's meant to show that options were so limited that some would accept that by not marrying for love, they would have an easier time finding themselves a match."

He nodded slowly, and his lips pursed as he thought over my words and planned how he wanted to keep the conversation afloat. "Okay. I think I understand what you are saying now." Wyatt only paused momentarily before continuing with his thought. "Do you think it's important to marry for love?"

"Of course I do." It quickly daunted me that he might feel another way if he asked the question, so worry leaped into my voice as I asked, "Why? Do you not think so?"

"It sounds like a good idea in theory, but you must admit it doesn't make sense." Wyatt hesitated. I watched his eyebrows pinch together as he planned out his next move. It was no secret how much I love romance novels and chick flicks, something he often made fun of, and he seemed to think he needed to tread softly around a topic I was sensitive to. "The entire matrimony system is flawed. Anyone can see that if they really look into it."

He let the conversation dance circles around me, but I would not do the same to him, so I went for the direct approach. "How is it flawed? Your parents are married and happy."

Wyatt seemed to have thought this over by the rapid progression of his words. "My parents pretend to be happy. My parents will tell everyone how happy and in love they are, but they always fight. You are still on the outside, so you haven't seen it; they still think they need to fake it around you, but if you stick around long enough, that will go away. Then you will be sworn into secrecy like the rest of us." He only paused to see if I would interject, but I didn't, so he kept going. "My dad thinks he's above everyone else, including my mom. How does that promote the idea of marriage to their children? Or make them want to follow in their footsteps?"

I hadn't heard him speak so intensely about anything before. "There are happy marriages out there. We have seen them before, even if we didn't get the pleasure of growing up underneath them." I tried to think of the people we mutually knew and how they acted with their spouses, but no actual happiness came to mind. My dad hadn't stuck around when my mom got pregnant, choosing to pop in and out when it was convenient for him. My grandparents acted like they were roommates, sleeping in separate bedrooms on different floors of their large house. "I can't think of any right now, but they are out there."

"Maybe you can't think of an example because there aren't any." He almost seemed disappointed in this, like he was baiting me to find the answer he was looking for. His eyes looked down at the pen and subconsciously started spinning again. It was as if he was forcing himself to keep his eyes on the spinning object.

A list started filtering through my mind of celebrities who managed to keep long-term relationships since the examples in our lives would not convince him. That probably only meant they were lying harder, but at least then I could have an example or two. My mom's favorite singing couple came to mind so fast that I screamed their names, "Tim McGraw and Faith Hill!"

He laughed at my desperation to convince him that love was possible. "Who are Tim McGraw and Faith Hill?"

"They are both country music singers. They have been married since the late '90s." I used the computer in front of me to pull up a picture of them for him to see them. There was even one comparing an image from their first year to one now; both had aged well. You could see how much time had passed, and how they looked at each other was so sincere you could feel it. I could only imagine how strong it would have felt if I had been near them when it was taken. "They seem to love each other; anyone can see that."

"So, you found one example out of millions of broken hearts and divorces?" He pushed the conversation further, searching for something in my words that he hoped I would say. "There will always be a needle in a haystack. One of us will be lucky enough to fall and land on it."

I went through my list once more and realized I knew of another couple, and this one he might know who they were. "Here is another example." I pulled up another picture on my laptop, flipping it around for him to see the screen.

He erupted into giggles when he saw who I had for my new example. "Snoop Dogg! You have got to be kidding me."

I flipped the computer back to me and read the headline posted over the picture of Snoop Dogg and his wife. "Snoop Dogg has been married to his high school sweetheart since 1997. They have three beautiful children together and are enjoying retirement, although we all anticipate new music now that he has returned to the industry." My face grimaced slightly when I said, "So what does that mean to you? If one of the most notable rappers in the world has been able to find and hold onto love since he was a teenager, then I believe we 'normal' people might actually get a shot at a real love story, even if it is fleeting."

I didn't know if the image of Snoop Dogg floating around in his head or my explanation helped him remember what Charlotte said to Elizabeth in the novel, but he did pass the test.

* * *

A maid dropped off drinks beside us on the patio table. I called after her a "thank you," but she walked away too fast to acknowledge my gratitude. She made quick work of passing from the kitchen to the pool.

I could understand how Caroline had gotten used to such treatment. It was thrilling to have someone wait on you. It made you feel close to a princess, especially when you grew up in a home like this one and when your last name was used to escape any problem you faced. I could see why Caroline acted the way she did when things didn't go her way.

"I am going to get in the pool. Do you want to join me?" Caroline asked as she layered another thick layer of tanning oil, her third layer since we came out here. While she was lucky enough to have gorgeous hair and beautiful eyes, she was forever envious of my tanning ability. In the time we had spent outside this week, I had already darkened my color by a shade or two, while she only proceeded to become slightly pink, although it would do me no good to point that out to her.

Caroline hoped to have a tan before our homecoming, which meant taking advantage of the sun while we still had it. We were on our fourth day in the water, and my tan lines were only becoming more prominent, which gave me a thrill of satisfaction now that Caroline made me realize how valuable it was to the girls at our school. Every day after school, she dragged us outside with our textbooks in tow, and we laid out on the loungers while we studied under the beating sun. After about an hour, she would declare we needed a break, and we would spend the next two hours floating in rafts on the water before returning to the loungers to continue studying. The cycle rotated on the same mental clock until the sun started to go down, and then we would throw our towels around our bodies and our textbooks in our bags to go inside for dinner.

I stood from the padded lounge chair, taking my drink with me while I sat in a white floaty raft that had become mine over the past week. The cool blue of the water was refreshing when mixed with the combination of the cold drink, and even better was the view of the basketball court, which was another reason Caroline wanted us to study outside by the pool.

Wyatt and his two best friends, Nolan and Kaden, also enjoyed the excellent weather by playing a pickup basketball game. My favorite part was that they had all decided that their shirts would only hold them back, so there were now three shirtless teenage boys who were impressively athletic that we had the pleasure of checking out.

While Caroline stared off at her brother's friends, my eyes were locked on Wyatt. I could see the three boys talking about something, and it seemed like they were talking about something more than basketball because of how animated their movements were. Wyatt and Kaden were waving their arms as if their words were not getting their point across.

"What do you think they are talking about?" I opened my thoughts to Caroline, hoping she had some insight since she was close to one of the three boys, as if living in the same house might give her access to his thoughts. "They've been talking for a while."

She wasn't looking at them like I was. Instead, she fussed with her red bikini to ensure the strings lay how she wanted them to. It was new, and she was excited to wear it; it was also something her parents did not know she owned, so she was taking advantage of their vacation. Caroline had become shockingly rebellious since the beginning of high school, and this was small compared to some of her other actions I had tagged along for. "I don't care, but I hope two of them are commenting on how good I look in my suit and that Wyatt won't say anything to our parents." She meticulously adjusted it as Kaden's eyes danced in our direction in response to something Wyatt asked him. "How do I look?"

"You look good. I like that color on you." We have played this game a million times now. It began when she felt insecure about something, so she baited a compliment out of me, which I happily obliged by telling her how good something looked, or how pretty or smart she was. My mom was the only one who ever told me how great I am, how beautiful and unique I am, and that I could take on the world, filling me with confidence. Her mom only did the opposite. MaryAnn had a talent for making both of her children feel small.

She twirled a single strand of hair between her fingers, inspecting it for split ends. It was her nervous habit, trying to ensure she stayed as perfect as possible. "I should have curled my hair or put some makeup on. The summer look is so not in right now, not that boys understand trends."

I didn't understand how a summer look wouldn't be in style during the summer. I knew better than to ask questions about fashion and style since it was a topic I knew so little about, and she was the reigning expert. Her light shone brightly, and I was happy to bask in her warmth.

"You were going to curl your hair to lay out by the pool?" I couldn't help but laugh a little at her. Caroline Calloway required male attention like the rest of us needed oxygen. It was mostly just for fun; it would only be dangerous if she cared for any of them, and thankfully, most of the time, she didn't. She loved that they were willing to chase her, but once they caught up, she was ready to pass on them quickly with the excuse of school or wanting to keep her priorities in line.

She twirled a blond piece of hair between her manicured fingers, using that to appear carefree, even though I knew she was fretting about her bikini and how it looked now that the boys were nearby and could potentially be looking at us. Caroline was calculated in her pursuit of their attention, preplanning her movements similar to the way her father did in a boardroom. She liked to pretend that she wasn't anything like him, but I saw his traits in both Caroline and Wyatt. "No, but it would look good. I guess it's a good thing I didn't with this humidity. It would have been gone by the time they looked over here." Caroline's eyes were trained in the same direction mine were, and we watched the boys end their game. She let out a slight sound of alarm when they started walking towards us; this was to ensure I was prepared even if I wasn't already watching. "Do you think they are going to join us?"

I wouldn't have guessed they would. Wyatt enjoyed keeping his life separate from his sisters whenever possible. Still, they kept walking in our direction, only pausing to discard the items from their pockets onto the loungers. "It looks like they might be." I tried to pull my eyes away, but it didn't seem possible with the way Wyatt's eyes met mine and stayed.

She dropped her sunglasses over her eyes so she could watch them without their knowledge. Caroline admired Nolan's and Kaden's walking; her head bobbed back and forth between the friends as if she couldn't decide which one she wanted to watch more. Their steps were almost in unison, like the opening of a cheesy movie to show that they were the hot guys we were destined to fall in love with. "If Wyatt says anything rude about my suit, I need you to divert his attention elsewhere. I know he will say something to Mom and Dad if he realizes they don't know about it. He got in trouble last week, and I know he's looking for a way to divert their attention off of him and onto me."

I hadn't realized how far I would take her statement until Wyatt and the boys joined us, all three using their basketball shorts as swim bottoms and jumping in the deep end before swimming over to where our rafts floated. Wyatt popped up beside me, grabbing the bottom of my raft and using it to hold his head above the water, although he was already at least six-three or four if the height comparison to my height of five-two had the math right and was more than capable of standing at full size in the pool. He turned his attention to his sister and gave her a once-over with a disapproving look. "Care, what are you wearing?"

Caroline faked a surprised gasp, pretending she hadn't predicted his question, "What do you mean? It's just a swimsuit." She gave him a batted-eye smile to try and sway him not to tattle to their parents. "Mom doesn't care what my swimsuits look like, you know that."

She wasn't lying; her mom didn't care what her swimsuits looked like when they fell between the general guidelines of modesty, and this suit was definitely outside those lines. MaryAnn let her kids get away with a lot, but Caroline's clothing was not one of them. She believed that everything her children did reflected how she and Steve appeared, and appearances meant a lot to them.

"I don't think she would appreciate you wearing that one, and I know Dad wouldn't if he saw you in it." He gave her a sharp, disapproving look. "You should put more clothes on. I can grab my t-shirt for you to wear."

I laid my hand across his arm, taking my job as the distraction seriously. His eyes turned to look at me with some surprise that I was making the first move, so I lowered my gaze and batted my eyelashes enthusiastically in the way I had seen Caroline do to the boys in our class. It felt foreign to do something like that with my body, but I pushed through with a smile. "Wyatt, what do you think of the ending to Pride and Prejudice?"

I was already outside my comfort zone in the black swimming suit Caroline had helped me pick out at the mall earlier this week. It was much less skin than Caroline showed, but it was much more than what I was usually willing to show.

"I thought it was good. You were right, Mr. Darcy and Elizabeth falling in love is the only way the book could end. I do think it's a cliche that they ended up together when Mr. Darcy was against it from the beginning. It seems like he changed a lot for her." His eyes went over me in a way they had never done before. It seemed like he was finally allowing himself to look at me as a girl and not as his little sister's best friend. His eyes paused on their second pass, and I felt a shiver come over me at his attention. "You look really good, Flick."

As far as sincere compliments go, it was subpar, but it was impressive on the level of praise a sixteen-year-old boy can give. I was flattered that he thought to say anything at all.

I let my hand stray from his forearm to his bicep, squeezing it and giving him a long look that I hoped was flirty. My experience with the male gender was just in the form of slight insults covered by jokes about how siblings treated each other, so this was something new for me. "Thanks, Wyatt. I'm glad you like it."

He stayed attached to my raft, floating on the water's surface, holding onto my legs. It wasn't the sun heating the pool anymore; it was how his forearms touched my skin. "If I knew you would be out here, I might have come to swim earlier."

Nolan and Kaden were messing around with a foam football, tossing it back and forth from one end of the pool to the other. It was clear that they were trying to make the other person drop the ball, forcing them to be the loser in the game they had created. Caroline was distracted watching them, so I knew the other people in the pool didn't care about what we were saying to each other, which had to be the only reason I flirted back. "I would have invited you, but then I wouldn't have gotten the opportunity to watch you play basketball."

He played football for our high school, but I had not seen him play anything else despite all the teams he participated on. He was a natural-born athlete, but Caroline had been honest in admitting that they often stayed away when their dad was home, and that was the only reason he had tried out for any of the other teams. Their dad was on a business trip this week, so they were hanging out at home. When he returned on Sunday, Caroline would suddenly want to spend time at my house, and I had no idea where Wyatt disappeared to when Steve Calloway was home.

"Do you play?" He gestured to the basketball court over his shoulder as if I didn't already know what we were discussing. "We could get out and play a round of horse. Caroline could work on her tan without you."

That sounded like the last thing I wanted to do, but I was willing to bet he wasn't serious, so I went along. "I don't think you could handle how good I am." The wink wasn't necessary, but I loved the smile he gave me when I did it. "I would give you a run for your money."

"You think you would be able to beat me?" Wyatt seemed surprised at my statement. I had the pleasure of watching many girls come up to flirt with him, and that was not anywhere near the response they usually received. Usually, he went in for the flirtiest response possible as his return, and I was thrilled to receive the same response. The balance of friendship and whatever this was somehow managed to be uneven, tipping towards the latter, and the way he spoke only furthered that idea.

A maid walked out and deposited a few sodas on the side of the pool. Wyatt reached over and grabbed two for us before anyone else could get the Dr. Pepper that I loved so much.

"I know that I would." I giggled as he ran the ice-cold can up my arm. A shrieking noise came out of me as he went up past my wrist. I could feel the hairs start to rise along my forearm. "I'm pretty good at basketball. I might even be better than you if you give me a second to warm up."

He reached up to tickle my sides, forcing even more shrieks and giggles to leave my mouth. The raft I was floating on threatened to tip me over each time we moved with the water. I kept expecting him to release his hold on the raft, but he continued holding on, keeping our bodies close. "Yeah, you think you're better than me?" His hands felt like fire against my bare skin, the touch lighting something inside of me that I wasn't expecting. "You think you could beat me? I would love to see you try, Flick."

"Oh, I bet you would." I knew he wouldn't make me get up and prove it so I could tell him anything I wanted. "I don't think so. If we went head-to-head right now, I know I would beat you. The saddest part is that it wouldn't even be that hard."

He gave me another deep look; the laughter behind his bright blue eyes was evident. I knew that he enjoyed teasing me, but this was more. "Maybe we should go to the court and see what you can do."

It was exciting even to think about being alone with him, even if it was something I would never entertain. Caroline wouldn't be able to handle me choosing to spend time with Wyatt over spending time with her, even if she was distracted by the boys. The sibling rivalry was ever present, both trying to possess something the other had.

I bounced my feet in and out of the cool blue water, splashing Wyatt. He enjoyed it, splashing me back. It was a game to him, mainly because it was just another thing to get a reaction from me.

Before we could plan to go anywhere, another maid brought the group some popsicles to combat the beating sun. We all gratefully took one. Wyatt used the condensation from the drink to make more lines up and down my arm, almost absentmindedly, as he spoke to Kaden and Nolan about next week's football game and the practices that would happen before.

Even if he wasn't looking at me, I could tell he was satisfied with getting a response from me. The shivers differed significantly from the heat, proving he had been there. Caroline continued to mess around with her bikini, hoping one of them would look over at her. They continued only to be interested in their game, even if it came second to their conversation with Wyatt.

"Maybe I should call Jessica over." Caroline was talking to me but seemed unable to sway her eyes away from her brother's friends. "She only works until three on Thursdays. She could come join us."

Jessica was just as boy-crazy as Caroline was, as they often walked circles around the parties we attended while I found myself standing near Wyatt and his friends. I thought they were better company, at least, over the rounds the girls chose to do around the room.

Wyatt followed his sister's lead, talking to Caroline while only looking at me. His can hadn't stopped in its voyage across the surface of my arm. "Yeah, that's a good idea. If she came over, I would feel like a fifth wheel."

His being the odd one out was a joke. It was conspicuous by how he attached himself to my side and how the other boys played with their inflatable ball. Caroline was the odd one out of this group.

Caroline pushed her raft to the side of the pool and rang the bell for the maid. The woman in her sharp black uniform looked out of place beside the carefree kids wasting the afternoon in the pool. "Will you call Jessica Chang and have her come over?"

"Of course, miss." The maid went off, obeying the command of her much younger boss.

"We need her here to make this into a party." Caroline returned to the rest of us with a satisfied smile, happy that her plan was coming into action. "Now, this is going to be fun."

Chapter 3

Bridal Shower

Caroline was wearing another expensive white bridal-themed outfit. It had been steamed to perfection by the two maids whose only job was to ensure her happiness; some of them had been employed by the Calloway's since we were teenagers, so they greeted me at the bedroom door with a friendly smile. Caroline's parents spared no expense for her wedding wardrobe, decking her out in the nicest outfits. It was similar to the 1800s debutante when their parents bought a wardrobe to display their daughter's dowry; this was identical to how Caroline's parents were taking this opportunity to show their wealth.

This outfit was a short white dress that she paired with a matching bow in her hair. The simple strappy white heels on her feet looked good, and the dress's intricate design was impressive. It had started to get colder, but she was clinging to the last of summer with her outfit and the location of her bridal shower.

She had asked everyone else in attendance to wear pastels to the tea party theme, which went with the butterfly garden we had decorated throughout the greenhouse. Caroline wanted a celebration different from the stiff party a bridal shower usually was. She especially wanted the party to fill her childhood fantasies, so we ordered special butterflies to fly around the greenhouse during our tea party. The color theme was a cute idea, although I regretted my decision to wear green, especially after one of Caroline's five-year-old cousins had run past me and informed me that I was the same color as the booger he had pulled from his nose this morning. That comparison only made me feel worse about myself and my choice to wear such a color.

I was hoping to wear it to stay on theme, and a small part of me chose that color so I could hopefully blend into the greenery around us. I was desperate to step back into the foliage and disappear entirely, especially after the interaction Wyatt and I had at the engagement party. I knew better than to let my heart get close to him again, yet somehow, I had still ended up in his arms. He was an addiction I could not allow myself to indulge in.

Jessica Chang, another survivor of our Riverside Prep education, ran around the greenhouse, helping my mom spruce up the plants and bring in a few hundred new ones. The whole point of having it in the greenhouse was that the plants were beautiful and would make an excellent backdrop for the photos. With the three of us, plus the house staff, running around, it was starting to come together as Caroline's vision for that event.

My fellow bridesmaid had made the smart move to wear a pink sundress. It was flattering against her long black hair and the delicacy of her pale skin. There was also no chance that a kid would come up and compare her to anything unpleasant.

After attending Harvard for her law degree, she worked as a lawyer in New York. Jessica didn't intentionally follow Wyatt to school, but they did get together once she got there, which had been hard for me to stomach. He had dumped me in high school so that he could date around in college, but I never would have guessed that he would start dating Jessica.

It had been years since they were together and even more years since Wyatt and I had broken up, but it still felt like a fresh wound when she showed up to be one of Caroline's few bridesmaids, although I tried to convince myself those feelings of jealousy weren't there. Mom suggested that I grin and bear it, and I loved Caroline enough to do just that.

Mom, Jessica, and I worked hard to ensure that the bridal shower would be the best party Caroline had ever seen while MaryAnn stood in the dining room sharing a drink with her two sisters. They enjoyed the title of hostess, especially when the team they hired could do all the important things without them having to worry; their only job was to appear gracious to the compliments that would come. It didn't take long to realize that martinis went down easy when you had no other stresses on your mind.

They were sloppy drunks, so one of the things on my to-do list was ensuring they were ingesting food between each cold olive-filled glass. I only hoped they could hold it together for conversations when the guests arrived.

While mom headed to the staff kitchen, Jessica and I stood at the front doors, welcoming all the guests after the staff escorted them to the greenhouse.

We had a gift table inside the door with the first ten guests' presents. A few staff members were directed to ensure the gift table looked full without appearing overfilled. It was a set job that only someone as wealthy as the Caloway's could warrant even having.

Everything was ready to go, but we were still missing the bride. Jessica shot a glance at the watch on her wrist. "Should we go get her?" It was ten past twelve, and most guests had already arrived. "She didn't tell me a set time. Did she talk to you about when she wanted to join us?"

One of Caroline's only stipulations regarding the wedding process was that she wanted to make an entrance to every party, which meant arriving fashionably late for every celebration. It forced an eye on her as if she was not already the center of attention, as much as we loved Caroline, everything about her screamed socialite except for her genuine heart.

"No, but I think you're right about going to get her." We planned for me to go into the house to get Caroline while Jessica announced the bride's arrival to the guests. She was much more comfortable in front of a crowd, so I was happy to hand over that job.

The path from the house to the greenhouse was paved with cobblestones and small lanterns that would light the way once it darkened. I had opted out of the heels Mom suggested and instead wore wedges, so thankfully, the flat bottoms gave me an advantage over the uneven walk.

"What are you doing out here?" Wyatt was coming down the path in the opposite direction, meeting me halfway between the greenhouse and the Calloway home. "Shouldn't you be down at the party? I thought you were the host."

"Yes, but I need to bring Caroline down. She wanted to wait until the guests arrived to make her big entrance." I explained what Caroline wanted as if he didn't know how she was or how the engagement party went. Wyatt was dressed in a polo shirt and another pair of khaki shorts. It was an outfit designated for golfing, and I could only assume that was where he was going since that had always been the Saturday routine for Steve Calloway for as long as I had known their family.

He chuckled softly, knowing his sister as much as I did. This was not something new for her. "I'm shocked she's not having you sprinkle fresh rose petals before each step as she makes her way down here."

That was something she would have done when we were teenagers, but that had thankfully changed as she matured, and there was only a tiny remanence of her selfish habits left. They only had reignited with the pressure and excitement of wedding planning. This was the most similar to MaryAnn Caroline had ever appeared.

"No, but Jessica is announcing her arrival, so everyone will anticipate her like she wanted." I could feel the corners of my mouth perk in a slight smile just thinking about Caroline's 'look at me' request.

"Jessica's here?" I watched him perk up instantly as his eyes seemed to sparkle with the words. "I'm going golfing with Richard and my dad. Maybe when I return, I will stop by the party and say hi."

The Wyatt that I used to know hated golfing. Steve forced him to go whenever he wanted to lecture him, so I knew better than to assume that was why he was smiling. "Golfing? You always hated golf."

He shrugged carelessly, "Well, a lot has changed since we were teens."

"Yeah, well, Jessica's inside the greenhouse if you want to stop by." I spit the words out, not trying to disguise my jealousy. Obviously not everything had changed since high school.

I didn't realize how much his interaction with Jessica would bother me until he talked about seeking her out. All I could think about was their pictures on social media when they started dating in college and how happy their smiles were with their arms wrapped around each other. It broke my heart, proving that I had not gotten over him like I wanted to. Caroline had tried to break the news to me gently, but that was hard to do when you were eighteen and still yearning for your first love.

He seemed to catch the change in my tone by taking a visible step back. "I need to meet the guys on the course. I'll have to stop by later." Wyatt leaned forward and pressed a gentle kiss to my cheek, something that was common for his social stature. It had been so long that my body must have forgotten him and how he forced my heart to patter and goosebumps to appear. "I hope you will be here when I get home; I want to talk to you about something."

Wyatt walked quickly back to the garage at the back of the property, probably searching for his old set of golf clubs, or maybe he had a new set. Adult Wyatt wasn't someone I knew, and there was no way I would know the status of his weekend habits or golf clubs like I once did.

I tried not to think about Wyatt Calloway as I raced for the house, trying to make up for the lost time by taking the stairs two at a time. As teenagers, Caroline and I had done it all the time, and my body remembered the movement like it was yesterday, even if I had to extend my 5'2 frame further than it normally went.

Care had always been taller than me by at least a few inches, but in the end, she was half a foot taller than I was. Care had ended up similar in height to a model and that was exactly how she looked now that she was dressed for the bridal shower. The white dress and the excess of pearls, that were currently in style, looked fabulous on her. Things that showed class and style were important to her.

Her newest spray tan was slightly orange, but I would never tell her that because it was a touchy subject we had hashed out enough times as teenagers. I could only hope that the greenhouse greenery would cancel it out. It was also not a secret that no one would say anything negative to the bride on her special day. Behind her back, this crowd would have negative things to say, but that wouldn't be the case if everything were perfect. If everything went right, there would be comments about what a princess she was and how everything went perfectly because of how much money her parents had spent on the day. If anything went wrong, they would use that to poke fun at her expense, shooting down the girl who appeared perfect and picking apart the day.

"Hey, everyone is here." I tried to sound as upbeat as possible, hoping to forget about Wyatt wanting to see Jessica. It seemed like the smile I had plastered onto my face wasn't as fake as it felt because she didn't seem to notice anything was wrong, but then again, she was in her own little world. "Are you ready?"

She looked one more time in the mirror, sticking out her tongue at me as our eyes caught in the glass. Her hands smoothed down the front of her sundress and adjusted her necklace until it lay flat against her skin. "How hammered is my mom?"

MaryAnn was pretty drunk despite my effort to keep her sober. The bride's mother and two aunts worked hard to ensure their martini glasses were never dry. It had to be a genetic trait that allowed them to drink in such a fashion since they never had a hangover or any issues the following day.

"She is barely hammered," The lie came easily since it was a lie to protect her. It would only stress her out to know that MaryAnn was drunk, running around talking to everyone at the party and probably embarrassing Caroline. It would have been better if she walked into the party without knowing. "By the time we arrive, she will probably have sobered up. I wouldn't worry about it."

It's funny what a decade of friendship does to how you know someone. I knew that hearing the state of her mother would make her anxious and sick to her stomach. I also knew she had trusted me to handle the day, including MaryAnn.

"Okay. I'm good. Let's get out of here." She shook away her nerves by doing a visible shake of her hands, then wrapped her arm around mine, heading to the door with a smile. "What is my Aunt Martha wearing? Is it hideous?"

MaryAnn came from money, and when she married Steve, she only came into more money, which was common among the elite. Her sisters stayed at the same wealth level they had been at before marriage, and although it was thousands above where my family financially stood, it was considered poor in the Calloways' eyes.

Martha often tried to bridge the gap between the sisters, choosing to wear last season's Gucci items to appear just as wealthy; she seemed to forget that last season's things in a crowd like this was just as bad as wearing something from a thrift store. That was the very reason MaryAnn had always dressed me before I went to any event with their family. My shoes from Walmart would not fit their high standards.

I played along with their game, "She is dressed in last season's clothes! After the party, you will have plenty of gossip to swap with your mom tonight." Gossiping was how they bonded, sinking their teeth in and ripping apart everything they found imperfect. That was how all the women in this crowd acted: sweet as pie to your face but desperate to sink a knife in your back.

Caroline wasn't usually that way. There was something about being near her mom, and she was constantly seeking her approval. It made her personality into something I didn't always care for. Once she was away from her mom, everything was okay again, and she returned to her usual kind and gentle personality.

My theory was that she was desperate to have something in common with her. She was fighting for a mother-daughter relationship like mine that Caroline would never have.

Caroline had voiced before that she was envious of the relationship between my mother and me. I understood because I was jealous that her dad was around for things, even if he was sometimes a jerk. Occasionally, I wondered if that was friendship, loving each other so much that even if you were jealous, you couldn't help but let those feelings slip away for the sake of your friend's feelings.

We got to the bottom of the stairs, and I helped her across the path. We were both grateful for my flat-bottom wedges since her heels were making for a less-than-graceful walk. "Did my grandma show up? Mom said she might be stuck in New York for the weekend, and I was kind of hoping that she would be."

"Yes, she is seated with a glass of wine in hand. It's going to be perfect." All of the Calloway women were nicest when they had a glass of wine in their hand, so I instructed the staff to keep white wine nearby.

Caroline laughed, instantly understanding what I was saying without me having to say anything about the mean older lady. "Make sure there is a glass ready for me too."

"Already on it." I laughed.

We got to the glass doors, and we could already hear the chatter from the crowd. Somehow, it felt similar to lions in the den waiting for their dinner. "I am so nervous. Why am I so nervous? I know these people."

"Because those women are monsters! They are waiting to eat us alive." We had both been on the negative side of their words enough times to understandably be nervous to go in there. We both did our nerve shake, moving our hands and arms until the jitters were out.

"Just think, you are the hottest thing ever to walk the earth! Not to mention the hottest thing to walk into that room."

Caroline blushed, and she let out a giggle. "You flatter me." She said, punching me lightly on the arm.

"Maybe, but it took your mind off of it." I pressed my hand between her shoulder blades and pushed her forward until she stood before the glass doors. We could see all the women on the other side, enjoying themselves while they waited. "Now, go celebrate yourself!"

She opened the door to the greenhouse, and cheers flew to our ears as the guests welcomed the bride. Jessica's voice rang out loudly, "Welcome to the future, Mrs. Chadwich."

Caroline waved to everyone while she walked to the makeshift stage, where Jessica was standing with a microphone. It was like watching a pop star grab a mic with how comfortable she was with it in her hand. "Thank you all for coming to my bridal shower today! It is an honor to have all of you here to celebrate with me.

Mom approached my side and slipped a glass of sparkling cider in my hand. "Take a sip. You look like you're going to be sick."

"Good call, I shouldn't drink. I need to keep a clear head as the butterfly releaser." I tried to sound as rational as possible even though what I was saying sounded ridiculous.

She pushed it towards me once more. "It's sparkling cider. You can handle your butterfly job just fine. Now, drink up."

I leaned my head to hers to whisper the dreaded question. "How is MaryAnn doing?"

Mom giggled as she glanced over to where the bride's mother sat. "She is drunk as a skunk, but I think she's keeping it as under the table as possible." Mom discreetly pointed to where MaryAnn was giggling with Martha. The two sisters found joy in something, and it wasn't Caroline's words. "Jessica got her to eat something when you went to get Caroline. Hopefully, she will keep it together long enough to get through this."

Caroline's mom and mine did not ever get along the way Caroline and I did. They were too different in personalities, which was probably why MaryAnn didn't handle it well when Caroline asked my mom to be her wedding planner. She didn't love the idea of handing over the reins on such an important day, wanting to use someone of higher class like those who had done her friends' daughters' weddings.

Caroline continued to thank her guests and encouraged them to eat the food and drink the champagne before stepping down from the stage to join the crowd.

"Is the plan still to let people eat and drink for 30 minutes before opening the presents? When do you want to release the butterflies?" I went off my checklist in my mind. Mom had the sheet pulled up on her iPad, but neither of us needed to look it over. We both memorized it long before today.

She immediately returned to work mode as if a switch had been flipped. "Let's make the announcement and do it now." Mom flew to the other side of the room as if lifted by the clouds and started directing Jessica, pointing to the stage for her to make the announcement. I followed along the side walls until I was behind the butterfly cage.

"We want to thank you again for coming here today to share in this moment with Caroline. We have a special surprise for you," Jessica said into the microphone with confidence I didn't possess. "Count down with me, three...two...one!"

With her enthusiasm, I lifted the arm of the cage and let the butterflies flood the room. There was a rush of orange and black as the monarch butterflies flew from the cage into the greenhouse. Everyone let out gasps as they took in the wonder before them.

The butterflies went around the room, randomly landing on the tables or even on top of the guests if they stood still long enough. I could see the same cousin who compared me to a booger celebrating as a butterfly landed on his plate.

Caroline walked in circles around the room, greeting each of the guests with a smile on her face. Her favorite part of her parties was the networking she got into, taking the opportunity to speak to each person individually. The guest list was a combination of family, friends, and multiple shareholders of several charities in the area. She had a talent for making everyone feel like they were the most important guest invited, which was the only reason she could get away with such a wide range of guests.

* * *

Wyatt still looked just as put together as he did when he left. You would never know he had been in the humid sunshine all day. It was unfair. "You look like you had a good day." He observed the room slowly, shifting his head from the left to the right to take it all in, although there wasn't much left to look at. The staff, Mom, and I had removed most of the decorations. I was still here to ensure the greenhouse looked as it had before the party, if not even better. Mom's golden rule was to leave a place better than when you found it.

"So do you." Even though he had mentioned stopping by, seeing him there was still a surprise. I was also curious to know if I still knew him as well as I thought I did, so I asked him the question that had been on my mind. "How was golfing?"

He smiled slightly, like he remembered something funny that had happened. "It was fine. Richard got stuck in the sand several times but held it together pretty well." He straightened the expression on his face, came deeper into the greenhouse, and changed the subject. "What did the guests think of the butterfly release? I know Care Bear was excited for it." He asked with a smirk while glancing curiously over my clothes.

I had traded my party dress for a pair of sweatpants and a T-shirt that had been his in high school. When we dated, quite a few of his clothes ended up at my house, and very few ever got returned to him. They were the perfect size for oversized shirts, although I kept them mainly because they reminded me of him.

I took a deserved break, leaning my hip against the table, and did some observations of my own. His polo fit his shoulders nicely, and he already had a soft tan line from where his sunglasses had sat on his face throughout the day. "It was a hit! They loved it, which made my mom very happy. The best thing was that your mom and grandma seemed pleased with it. I don't have to tell you how tough of critics they can be." I watched how he shifted on the balls of his feet in a nervous pattern I was used to. Knowing he would never tell me, I knew better than to ask him what he was thinking, so I changed the subject. "If you're looking for Jessica, she's not here. She already went home."

He chuckled under his breath, almost in surprise. "No, I came in here looking for you."

"Me? I thought you were trying to catch her when you came back. Didn't you say you wanted to come say hi?"

My frustration was thick, but he didn't seem to care.

Wyatt just rolled his eyes to go with his response. "No, I said that I *might* stop by to see her. That was a possibility, but I was *definitely* going to come find you." He stepped closer until he was close enough to reach out and slip his finger into the armhole of my shirt. Wyatt played with the frayed edges, probably remembering each of the small rips it had and how they got there when it had been his. "I can't believe that you kept this after all this time. I figured it had ended up at a second-hand store when we broke up."

There had been plenty of times that I thought about throwing it out. There were also plenty of times it had been thrown into a good-will bin before rescuing it again. There was something about the stretched-out, worn green fabric that fit just right, and even if he hadn't worn it in over a decade, the shirt still managed to smell like him. That combination, plus the memories, kept it in my closet.

At my mom's house, I had a box hidden beneath my childhood bed full of things Wyatt had given me, including a few of his shirts. I hadn't opened it in years, but I knew the contents like they were laid out before me since they were all mementos of our time together that I could never let go of.

"I figured it was a good top to get dirty in." I tried to brush it off with the shrugging of my shoulders. I should have probably worn something else, especially since I knew there would be a possibility of running into him. "I forgot I had it until I found it at my mom's house this week when I was getting stuff ready for the bridal shower."

It was a lie; the shirt had come to college with me and had followed me to the small apartment I kept above my bakery. It also ended up in my hamper every laundry cycle, ready to be folded and placed back at the top of my drawer.

"It looks good on you." His fingers continued playing with the edge of my shirt, and I loved how his fingers brushed against my body; his heat radiated against mine, and I relished the sensation. "I'm glad that you kept it."

I was glad I kept it too, even if it was only for this moment. There was a look in his eyes I had never seen before; it looked something like longing. "Did you come here to help me clean up? I'm not going to lie; I could have used the help an hour ago. Now I'm basically done."

He laughed as my words seemed to jump him out of his daze, shaking his head slightly and returning his attention back to my face instead of my shirt. "No, we just got back. I was actually on my way to the house to shower. I was surprised to see the lights were still on out here, so I came in to turn them off." He moved away from me, but not far. Wyatt stepped enough away that I lost the feeling of the warmth I felt with him near me, but he leaned against the table beside me. It was familiar, just like so many of his movements were. "Flick, I've wanted to talk to you about the engagement party and the moment I feel we had."

The moment we had stayed in my mind, even if it had been a few months since then. I had played it up in my mind that it was a fantastic moment, but I also had talked myself down that it was just a fleeting moment between two people who once had feelings for each other. Every day, I seemed to struggle with which one I felt it really was.

"We didn't have a moment." I shook my head softly, still taking the time to watch his reaction. I could only hope that my denial sounded confident.

"Flick, you know that isn't true." He bumped his hip against mine and gave me an irresistible smile. "You can't deny it. We had a moment, and it was a good one."

A scoff came quickly from my lips, and my body pulled away from his before I could control either action. "A good one?"

Wyatt let out a huff of frustration, and his hands moved furiously as he spoke. I was getting to him like I had so many times before. We had a habit of getting underneath each other's skin. "I should have known you were going to deny it. That is just like you to stomp down any feelings you have for me and pretend they aren't there."

No matter how confident he was, that wasn't true. I had changed a lot in the last eight years.

"There is nothing to deny because nothing happened." I tried to sound confident, but my voice still wavered. "We were there to celebrate Caroline. Nothing more."

He moved so fast that suddenly we were face to face. His eyes stared into mine, and it caused a rush to go down my spine, especially when his hands fell onto my hips. "Go on a date with me, Flick." He said it almost as a challenge. He looked deeply at me, trying to read me as he spoke. "I will pick you up, take you out, and we will have a great time. I think that is the only fair way to know that you are serious when you tell me that there is nothing between us."

"Wyatt, you're being ridiculous! We would just be wasting our time."

"No, I'm not." He was deadly serious; I could tell by the slightly raised eyebrows, and how his breath labored each time he tried to take more in. His grip on my hips tightened like he was afraid I would make a run for it if he wasn't careful. He was right to be wary; I was a flight risk. "Go on a date with me, and by the end, if you can tell me that you feel nothing, then I will back off, and we can just be friends."

The lie fell quickly from my lips. "I can tell you that now. There was no moment between us. There is nothing between us."

He gave me a devilish grin that melted me further. "If that was true, you would have thrown my shirt away. And the Flick I know would go so she could prove me wrong." His eyes trailed over my body, going from head to toe, then back up as if to ensure he didn't miss anything else. "I'll pick you up tomorrow at eight."

And then he walked out, leaving me staring at his fleeting figure, wondering what had just happened and wondering what I was going to do about it.

Chapter 4

Junior Year

Wyatt motioned for me to be quiet by pressing a stiff finger to his lips, although his smile showed me that he was barely containing his giggles. "You have to be quiet." He caught me as I missed a step on the tight staircase. Their house was so old; it was considered historic and had a staff staircase, which we were taking advantage of now to sneak up to his bedroom. Because it was behind the walls, it was narrow with small stairs, and I had tripped more than once with only the use of our cell phones for light. "If you wake up my parents, we will be in so much trouble."

Even though he was giggling, he wasn't kidding. I could only imagine Caroline's reaction, knowing that Wyatt and I were sneaking around behind her back. She could barely handle it when our friends at school had something going on that she was left in the dark about. It would be considered betrayal that Wyatt and I kept anything from her.

I didn't even know how it happened or how we got here, although I know that would not fly as an excuse to anyone.

My best friend lived in a world where everyone and everything had a reason behind what they were doing. She lived in a world where almost everything was perfect, which was why she was perfect or, at least, believed she had to be.

Caroline was Barbie, and this was her dream house.

We grew close as Wyatt and I studied every afternoon alone in the Calloway's kitchen. I enjoyed spending time with him; he was funny and kind when he wanted to be. Spending that time alone with him allowed him to open up in a way that was different than what he showed the rest of the world. I felt privileged to see him that way, like it was only a side of him for me. Working alone with him allowed him to be open with me regarding his dyslexia and the challenges it had given him, which only continued to bring us closer.

"Did you remember the popcorn?" I asked him since his hands were without the salty treat I craved. I pulled on his tan arm and gave him my version of puppy dog eyes. In my opinion, they were nothing special since they were dull and brown, but I hoped they would do the trick. "Wyatt, this is a big deal. We can't have a movie night without popcorn." I playfully whined.

"It's already in my room." He gave a confident smile, satisfied that he had already prepared for my request before I had even asked for it. "Don't worry. I knew you would want some, so it's popped and waiting just for you. I also have Swedish fish waiting for you in my mini fridge."

He thought it was weird that I enjoyed eating the fish-shaped candy as cold as possible; I even went as far as to keep a small bag in my freezer for emergencies. I loved that he remembered and had made sure there was some ready for me, especially since this movie night had been spontaneous. That could only mean he had put them in there a while ago, or this movie night was not as spontaneous as I thought.

Wyatt opened the door to the hallway, peeking his head out to ensure no one was coming down the hall that would see us. He made silly signals with his hands like a spy on a secret mission might do. He then whispered. "The coast is clear; we just have to hurry. We don't want Caroline to hear us."

The two of us darted down the hall as quickly and quietly as possible. He swiftly pushed me into his room, following behind me quickly and closing the door as silently as possible. He leaned against it and sighed in relief; you would think we had just pulled off the heist of the century instead of sneaking from one side of the hallway to the other.

"Do you think anyone saw us?" I was just as nervous as he was that we would get in trouble, but I was excited to be sneaking around with Wyatt, and it gave me a rush of butterflies. I would happily risk Caroline's wrath just to be alone with him.

He shook his head, awkwardly standing there with a misplaced smile. I knew why he acted so strangely since I was also acting differently from normal. This was uncharted territory for both of us, and we knew that if we crossed the line now, there would be no going back.

"I don't think so." Wyatt pressed his ear against the door and seemed satisfied when there were no noises on the other side. He turned back, avoiding my eyes as he spoke. His hand gestured to the rest of the room in the way of an invitation. "Do you want to..."

Wyatt trailed off quietly, and while he gauged what to say next, I observed his room. It was the first boys' room I had ever been in, and it wasn't what I expected. Wyatt had a TV mounted on the wall that faced in the direction of the couch. Caroline had a similar layout to her room, so I was familiar with it. Both bedrooms had a sitting room, a private bathroom, and even a minibar, then a short hallway to where their actual bedroom started. They only needed a stove to make their large suite into small apartments.

He had taken the time to clean or at least directed a maid to do it for him because it was immaculately clean for a teenage boy. Caroline hadn't been subtle about how messy Wyatt usually was.

I noticed that not only had he cleaned up, but he had also stacked a few pillows for us to lean against and had piled up blankets. The ottomans had even been pulled to the edge of the couch for our legs to rest on.

He struggled to find his words, so I finished for him. "Should we sit down and start the movie?"

The movie night idea was created when he informed me that he had never seen the classic movie *The Princess Bride*. It was my favorite, and he didn't catch it when I would quote the film during our study sessions. The only solution for that would be obviously for him to watch the movie.

I didn't think I would get a text from him the same day requesting to watch it tonight, but I was thrilled when I did.

Mom was working late and didn't care when I went to the Calloway house, although that was when I went to hang out with Caroline. I doubted she would be as okay with it if she knew I was hanging out with Wyatt, especially in his room, so I left those details out when I told her I was going over.

We sat on the couch, but surprisingly, he sat on the opposite end. It was as far away as he could possibly be while still remaining on the same couch.

I didn't expect him to act so strangely, but the awkwardness was endearing. Typically, we were comfortable with each other, but not today. Something about this had pushed us into a situation that no longer felt like our usual friendship.

Wyatt reached for the remote and pulled up the movie. Just as he was about to push play, I reached over to stop him. The brushing of our hands went off with a buzz of electricity, and a quiver in my voice shocked me as I asked. "Should we turn the lights off? Or pull out the snacks? Once we start, there will be no stopping. This is *The Princess Bride* rules."

He laughed a little under his breath to ease the tension we were both feeling. "Let me grab the popcorn and your Swedish fish." Wyatt hurried to the counter to grab our snacks, turning around to produce a large bowl of popcorn and a large cup covered with condensation. "I put the bag of Swedish fish in here with ice around it. I hope it will keep it cold for you. I wasn't sure how you usually keep them cold."

I took the cup from him, thanking him with a smile, and quickly reaching for a gummy fish. When it met my teeth, I knew my face showed how much I enjoyed its cold sensation. "This is perfect." I ate another one and enjoyed how his eyes watched my movements. "Thank you for doing this for me."

He sat closer the second time but conveniently placed the popcorn bowl between us so we wouldn't touch. "Do you want a blanket?" He asked, "I know you said you like a blanket when watching a show, so I stole this one from Caroline's room."

It was still September and shockingly warm outside, but I would never turn down a blanket when watching a movie. I could feel a blush rush to my cheeks as I enthusiastically nodded. He had put a lot of effort into remembering what I preferred. "That would be great. I love the combination of the warm blanket and the chill of the cold fish."

He covered my legs with a blanket from the pile he had created. His forearm brushed against my bare legs, and I felt an entirely different chill go through me. Our nervous smiles met, and my eyes conveyed my gratitude.

He turned the light off, and we started the movie. Although he did not relax, his entire body remained tense, and he didn't lean back against the couch. Watching Wyatt like this, I couldn't relax either.

As we watched the grandpa walk into his grandson's bedroom, I turned to look at him, taking in the sharp lines of his profile and the way his long hair lay across his forehead. He startled me when he spoke. "Stop looking at me."

He hadn't turned his head but somehow saw me watching him. "I'm not looking at you. I just happened to glance in your direction when you caught me. It was a coincidence."

"*Sure.*" He said it obviously sarcastically to show that he didn't believe me.

In a weak attempt to change the subject, I reached over and

threw a handful of popcorn into my mouth. I didn't bother to swallow before saying, "Yum, it's so buttery!" so the words came out muffled.

He let out another laugh, using that noise to disguise his body shifting as he moved closer to the center of the couch. "Is there a rule against talking in the movie too? Or just against pausing it?" He asked as he subtly moved closer once more. He lifted the remote in the direction of the TV, obviously asking if he could pause it.

"Oh, both. Definitely both. Since this is your first movie experience with me, I will give you a one-time pass." My mom and I took our movies very seriously, and I was bringing that same energy here today. The two of us planned our snacks, our popcorn, and which Chinese restaurant to get takeout from, and then devoted our Saturday nights to movie marathons. "Do you have any questions? Comments? Maybe some concerns that need to be addressed before we continue?" I asked sarcastically.

Wyatt rolled his eyes dramatically, pausing the movie and turning his body to face me directly. There was a shift in the energy in the room now that he was acting so serious. "No." He leaned forward, moving a hand to brush my hair away from my face. "I won't be able to focus if I don't do this first?"

His hands stayed on my face, pulling himself in until his lips landed on mine. It was sweet and perfect as I felt a rush of fireworks erupt between us.

As far as first kisses went, this one would be discussed for the rest of my life. His lips were soft but not slippery with ChapStick.

Wyatt broke our kiss but kept his face close to mine. His fingers played with my hair, teasingly touching the piece closest to my face and tugging it softly. "You have no idea how long I have wanted to kiss you."

I liked that he thought about kissing me because I had also thought about kissing him. The thought of kissing him constantly rotated through my mind, intensifying each time he gave me a teasing smirk. "I'm glad you did." I smiled, "I've wanted to kiss you, too."

He released me slowly and leaned back against the couch, leaving me to do the same. Wyatt reached for the remote, turning back on the movie to fill the silence that now plagued the room.

Neither one of us moved for the duration of the movie unless it was to reach into the popcorn bucket, each of us taking choreographed turns to ensure that our hands never touched.

There was now a static energy buzzing between us. I wanted to reach over and kiss him again but was nervous to make the next move, so I sat silently while the movie played before us.

The only time the silence broke was when Wyatt quietly chuckled at the movie; he especially enjoyed the scenes with Andre the Giant and would laugh when the actor would make a joke.

I nervously chewed on my gummy fish, no longer cold, not allowing myself to enjoy my favorite movie. I was too intensely focused on how close we were sitting and the heat that radiated off his body.

Wyatt reached out and grasped my hand, taking it from where I had it lying on the couch between us. There was a thin layer of sweat, providing me with the knowledge that he was just as nervous as I was.

The movie started coming to an end. It is the part of the movie where Westly lies on the bed and saves Buttercup from killing herself. "Of course, he came to save the day," Wyatt said enthusiastically, cheering for the story's hero. "I knew he was always a good guy; they deserved each other."

"And what makes them deserve each other?" I prompted him further, trying to understand what he was thinking. "She could have been a princess. Humperdinck is a coward; she could have avoided his wrath and had it all."

Wyatt scoffed, looking down at me like I was crazy. "You and I both can see the way they look at each other. You can't fake something like that; its true love."

"I thought you didn't believe in true love." I thought about our conversations in the kitchen when only the idea of Snoop Dogg and his wife made Wyatt even contemplate the idea of a lasting love.

He leaned in closer, taking a second opportunity to kiss me as the narrator spoke. "Since the invention of the kiss, there have been five kisses that were rated the most passionate, the most pure. This one left them all behind."

Wyatt chuckled at the irony of the movie and our timely kiss. "Make that six kisses. Maybe I will start to hear your argument that it could be true." And kissed me one more time.

* * *

"Why have you been acting so weird today? You keep staring at the door." Caroline snapped at me. This was the fourth time I had asked her to repeat herself as she talked about homecoming plans and who she hoped would ask her. "You look like you are waiting for someone to burst through the door."

She wasn't wrong. I had been nervously staring off at the living room door, anticipating Wyatt coming home. We hadn't spoken since our movie night, and I was anxious how things would be between us now that we had kissed.

I had half expected him to call me or text me. I figured that we would do something to acknowledge that we could consider our movie night a date, but he never did.

A small part of me also considered never walking into their house again, switching schools, and avoiding him forever the longer it took for him to say anything.

I could have avoided their house, at least a little longer, if Caroline hadn't pouted when I suggested going to my house. Their dad was away on a business trip for the weekend, and her mom was getting her second-nose job, so their house was empty. The empty house was a detail I spared from my mom when I asked her if I could spend the weekend at Caroline's.

"I just want us to get this done, and I don't want any interruptions." We were working on a math project and were supposed to use the dimensional math we had learned in class to make the floor plan of a house, complete with a diorama. Caroline liked to hide it, but she was a math whiz, so her part, over half the assignment, was done quickly while I had spent the last hour working on my part. Not only was I lacking in math skills, I was distracted by Wyatt coming home.

Although she was doing more work now, I figured it would be even out in the end since there was a good chance I would be working on the diorama alone. Caroline got distracted easily when it was something she considered boring, and this fell into that category. The supplies had been supplied for us courtesy of her staff, and if I hadn't dug my heels in, Caroline would have probably had a staff member do the entire thing for us.

Caroline snapped me out of my thoughts. "Stop, it's freaking me out. It's like a boogie man will jump out, and you are the only one prepared." She said it in a carefree tone. She had no idea how on the nose her comment was.

Wyatt did currently feel like the boogie man.

If he had told Caroline what we had done, she would not have been happy and would have forgiven him long before she ever forgave me; this was something I was all too aware of. It felt like I was walking on eggshells, constantly aware of each step I took.

I pulled my attention away from the door and focused on her, remembering the conversation before she called me out again. "So, do you want Kaden to ask you out? What is Wyatt going to say about that?"

It was no secret that Wyatt didn't want either of us dating any of the guys on his team, especially those he considered his best friends.

Caroline didn't seem bothered by her brother or his wrath; instead, she almost seemed to see it as a challenge. Her eyes got that devilish glimmer that the Calloway siblings both shared. "Oh, he is going to ask me. I have been dropping hints all week that I am still dateless, and I see it as his southern duty to make sure I don't stay that way."

Caroline would never ask a guy herself to dance, but she had no problem with dropping hints that he needed to ask her. I could only imagine what the poor guy was thinking, getting stuck between his best friend and his best friend's sister. I was on the flip side, and the sympathy I had for him came in waves.

A clatter of noise startled both of us as Wyatt and the very best friend we were discussing came tumbling into the kitchen. They looked just as surprised as we did to see them there.

"I thought you were going to Felicity's house this weekend." It sounded like a question, but it was more of an accusation that hinted that Wyatt wanted me there about as much as I wanted to be there.

Caroline scoffed and dramatically rolled her eyes at her brother. "No, just because Steve and MaryAnn are gone doesn't mean *you* are in charge."

The siblings only called their parents by their first names when they were gone. They wouldn't dare call them that to their faces. Although it was almost as if they felt they were strangers, people assigned to be their keepers.

Wyatt gave her a similar annoyed response. "No, Nolan, Kaden, and I are having a party tonight, so the two of you need to get lost. We can't have underclassmen at our party."

"And why can't we come to your party? We have just as much right to come to your party as anyone else." He went to interrupt, but she was on a roll and would not let him cut in. "You can't use the excuse of no underclassmen either. I know you will invite Ansley and Everly, not to mention the entire volleyball team, regardless of their status."

They stared down at each other, squaring off for control of their home and the freedom of their parent's absence. I kept my eyes trained on my hands in my lap, and I knew Kaden was smart enough to avert his eyes.

Wyatt conceded faster than I thought he would, presenting her with a compromise instead of continuing the argument. "You can stay for the first two hours, and then you are going to your room, and not coming out until the morning."

She seemed to contemplate that for a second before giving him her counteroffer. "Three hours, and you have a deal."

He extended his hand, allowing her to shake it to cement their deal. "Fine, but under no circumstances are you drinking."

"What!" She exclaimed in outrage. "You are being ridiculous. Of course, we will drink, it's a party."

"I am not going to risk you drinking and getting yourself into trouble; besides, it isn't worth even having a party if I will have to babysit you all night." I knew him well enough to know that he was serious about this one, and he would do whatever was necessary to ensure she followed his rules.

I heard their hands slap together as they agreed to the deal, and I took this as my allowance to raise my head and join the conversation. Kaden did the same, and we gave each other a sympathetic look at dealing with the Calloway's.

"Party starts at nine, and that is when your timer starts, so don't be late." Wyatt's eyes cut over to mine, but only briefly before he walked away, shouting back at us. "I don't want to see you with any guys at the party, or I will drag you out myself."

I wasn't sure which of us he was directing that comment to, but I kept my face as flat as possible so as not to give away anything to Caroline as she looked back at me with an offended expression. "Can you believe the nerve of that guy?"

Kaden remained in the kitchen, digging into the pantry, and came out, giving us a sympathetic smile and a handful of snacks in his hands. "I will try to convince him to give you an extra half hour."

As he took off after Wyatt, Caroline started bashing her brother. "Can you believe the nerve of the two of them? An extra thirty minutes! What is that supposed to be? A solution to the bedtime my brother feels like he can put over me? I am not a child! I have as much right to be here as he does."

I tried to calm her down, but she didn't care to entertain any of my solutions, mainly because they were to avoid the party altogether. After thirty minutes, I convinced her that we should finish our project before any other decisions were made regarding the party.

After humoring me for an hour, she was back to the party and how she would get more time. My favorite of her complicated ideas was to sneak into the party in disguise, her in a brunette wig and me in a blonde.

"I'm done with this. Let's go to the mall and look for some clothes for the party tonight." Caroline helped me gather our papers, tossing them back into our bags before reaching for her keys. "Don't pout. We haven't gone to the mall in forever because you hate it, so you owe me."

She wasn't wrong; she had taken my feelings about the mall to heart. Caroline had chosen to go online for most of her shopping ventures while we floated beside each other in the pool. She often complained that it didn't give her the same satisfaction as the swinging of shopping bags as we walked from one end of the mall to the other.

I conceded, agreeing to go with her to the mall as long as she promised we could finish our school project tomorrow. She rushed me to the back door and out to their garage, dialing the number for their chauffeur since it was apparent that Wyatt would not drive us anywhere, even if we begged.

The driver turned on the radio, using it as a way to buffer any conversations between us and his ears. Caroline watched him momentarily, ensuring he couldn't hear us before going over her party plans. "I think we should stop at a shop that sells wigs. Once we go for the allotted time, we go back upstairs, change our clothes, and throw the wigs on. We then wait a few minutes. By the time we return downstairs, the boys will be so drunk they will have no idea we snuck back in."

I was surprised she wasn't rubbing her hands together or cackling like an evil genius. She looked proud of her plan. "I don't think we will want to spend any more time at their party. We'll probably be over it by then." I racked my brain for another excuse to escape it but came up short, so I began to plead instead. "What about a spa day tomorrow instead of a party tonight? It's been forever since we did that."

She loved a spa day, which I tended to avoid unless I was trying to stay on her good side.

Caroline didn't seem to care about my generous offer. She only rolled her eyes at my pleading and pulled her phone out to google the stores at the mall as if she hadn't been there a million times. "I have never been allowed to attend a party before today. That's all people will talk about next week. These parties are considered the parties of the century, and it's at my house! It is as if we are hosting it. This will make us rise even higher on the popularity list." Her thumbs rapidly flew across the screen, pausing only when she looked up with a serious look. "We have to go and experience it at least once in our lifetime if we want to be somebody."

Caroline had a fantastic skill of making everything seem like life or death, that missing this one party would change the entire sequence of our lives. I would be one to argue that a high school party did not have that much power over anyone. I knew this was not what she wanted to hear; Caroline would just want me to go along with her plan, so I stopped arguing. I have a terrible habit of always giving in to her.

I plastered a big, bright smile on my face and reached over to squeeze her hand. "You're right. This will be so fun, and they will never figure out we snuck back in."

She seemed content now that I was on board with her plan and put her phone down in her lap, giving me her full attention and a wide smile. "How about I go red, and you go blonde? And if you like it, then we can get it dyed tomorrow. I have my mom's hairstylist on speed dial."

I reached up for my mousy brown hair and gripped it tightly, as if she would reach across the car and start hacking it away if I wasn't careful. "How about we just start with the wigs and see how we feel?"

The driver pulled up to the mall and let us out. Caroline almost seemed rejuvenated just to be at the mall again and walked with a skip to her step. "I texted Jessica, and she is inviting some of her brother's college friends."

I nodded in agreement, knowing I had already lost the battle and it would be better to follow along. "Okay, we can do that. Where do you want to look first?"

Caroline rushed me towards the first store on the left and immediately started going through the clothes rack. "We need to find you a dress in pink. That is what will look best with your tan." She was obsessed with our color palettes, deciding what colors would be best for our skin, and used that to dress me like her personal Barbie. "Here, go try this one on."

She pushed me toward the dressing rooms, and I happily complied because that was easier than fighting with her. The attendant opened up a room, and I hurried to throw the first dress on, ignoring the stubble on my legs with the hope that I could steal a shower before the party if she was going to force me into wearing a dress.

"How does it look? Come out here. I want to see you!" Caroline shouted at me as she entered the dressing room hall. I stepped out and took in her reaction as her jaw dropped. Her hands came up to clap in celebration, proud of the treasure she had found. "That makes you look so hot! I knew it would be perfect for you."

I turned around to check myself out in the mirror, and I felt satisfied that I did look amazing. The baby pink color helped there to be a blush to my cheeks and a shine to my skin; it also somehow managed to pull a few caramel highlights out of my ordinarily dull brown hair. "Does this mean we are done shopping?" I turned back to her and asked her with a hopeful smile.

Caroline scoffed, not happy that I already wanted to leave. "No, we need a second dress for your blonde wig." She thumped her finger against her lips in thought, the evil look returning to her eyes. "I think we'll find you a green one next. I still need to find something for me."

I stayed in the dressing room, trying on each dress she threw over the door, and kept my complaints to a minimum. I would change my outfit while she impatiently tapped her foot, waiting to see how it looked. Somehow, while I tried on dresses, she had also gone out and found two dresses for her to wear to the party.

I came out in a skintight baby blue dress, an option way out of my comfort zone, and gave a silent breath of relief as a satisfied smile came across her face. It was a clear sign that we finished this portion of our shopping adventure. Caroline gathered the dresses she decided against and took them to the attendant, happy to let her put them away.

"Hurry and change. We need to find shoes, and we also need to find you a foundation that matches your skin tone." She bossed me around while I rushed to change back into my clothes. "We should also look for some necklaces. I think our alter egos need jewelry to complete their look."

I hurried to throw my clothes back on and lace up my dirty white Converse before I raced out after her. In my hand, I clutched the two dresses she deemed appropriate. A small part of me feared if I parted with them for even a second, we would have to go through the options all over again, and that wasn't something I could handle or wanted to go through.

Caroline rushed me to the cash register, using her dad's Amex card to pay for our dresses. I tried to cover up my surprise as I took in the price; this was something that she didn't even bat her lashes at despite its large number. Somehow, the cost of our outfits for one equaled a month's grocery bill.

"Let's go look for shoes." She grabbed onto our shopping bags, and I trailed behind her. As soon as we found a store that sold shoes that she approved of, we went to the back of the store where the heels were held. Her hands immediately went shuffling through the boxes on the shelf, and she handed me options in my size, all while ordering me to try them on.

"I don't need shoes for tonight." I tried to reason with her, especially as my eyes racked over the price and the height, fearing both were outside of what I could handle. "I don't walk well in heels, you know that. I think it would be better if I wore my own shoes, especially if we are adding in alcohol."

I wasn't planning on drinking at this party, but it was the only argument she might agree with.

Her nose curled in disgust. "You are not wearing those ratty tennis shoes when Jimmy Choo's is an option."

"How about one pair? I will wear the Converse when we are at the party as ourselves since that is more authentic to my personality. Then, when we switch, I will throw on a pair of heels. No one would ever expect that from me, which will only further the argument that it's not us." I rattled off the words, and she pursed her lips, listening to me even if it was not making her happy.

"Fine, but that means you let me do your hair and makeup for both looks. No arguments." She negotiated, and I happily accepted it with a shake of her hand. "Now, if you are wearing the pink dress first, we will need to find some silver heels to go with the blue dress and a magic shoe eraser to make those at least somewhat look white again."

Caroline dove back into the racks, determined to find the perfect pair of shoes if she could only pick one. One of the store employees walked up and offered to help, but she knew the store better than anyone employed there and waved them off.

My phone went off in my pocket, alerting me to the text I had just received; Caroline was distracted by her hunt, so I knew she wouldn't care if I pulled it out.

Wyatt: Are you really going to come to this thing?

Felicity: Caroline wants us to.

Wyatt: That's not answering the question.

I didn't know how he wanted me to answer it. If I told him we were going to the party, he would not be happy, especially if he knew what Caroline was planning. He would also hate if I lied to him and then showed up to the exact place he was trying to keep us away from.

"Okay, I'm done." Caroline pulled my attention back to the store. She had three boxes of shoes in her hand and a proud smile at what she had found. "Let's take these up to the counter."

This time, I ignored the price as she swiped the card, knowing that I would feel better about putting the shoes on if I could pretend they were from Payless and cost less than twenty dollars, even if that wasn't true.

She handed me a few bags to carry, and we walked down the mall aisle. I decided to approach the subject she wouldn't be happy with. "So, what will we do if Wyatt figures it out?"

Caroline steered us ahead towards a jewelry counter. "He's not going to figure it out. You need to stop worrying so much."

I held my hands up in mock surrender. "I just don't want this to turn into a fight."

Somehow, she managed to distract me enough that I calmed down and got into the shopping spirit. Caroline picked out a simple necklace for each of my looks.

It wasn't long before our arms overflowed with shopping bags, finally when Caroline decided we could be done. I was even more relieved when the driver picked us up, and the heavy bags were stowed away in the trunk.

"We'll go in and sneak our bags past Wyatt. Then, we will get ready with our first outfit. Once there is a good turnout, we can go downstairs and do the party scene for our allotted time. When the time is up, we will go upstairs and change into our other outfits, change our makeup, and put on our wigs." Caroline commanded as if we were soldiers on our way to war instead of two teenagers who wanted to sneak into a party. "At that point, we will have been gone long enough that Wyatt will have forgotten that we were ever there. We will turn a movie on in my room and lock the door behind us so that it sounds like we are in there if he thinks about it and tries to check on us."

We got to the house, and Caroline flew up the stairs, her adrenaline fueling her burst of energy. Once the door to her bedroom was closed, she dumped the bags of clothes onto the bed and directed me to do the same. Her hands sorted our purchases into piles, one for our alter egos and the one we needed to get into now.

"Go shower and wash your hair while I finish getting this ready." She directed me in her tone and severe expression that showed she meant business.

I raced to the bathroom, happy to obey and get a second to myself. I had used her bathroom to shower often, mainly after football games, and she had bought the soaps that I liked. I even had my own razor, which was a blessing to change the status of my stubble-covered legs. When I had scrubbed, shaved, and shampooed to the point of being puffy and red, I exited the shower. There was a plethora of hanging towels, so I grabbed one to cover my body and one to wrap up my wet hair.

Exiting the bathroom, I was then put into the small hallway of her room, and it just happened to be where Wyatt was standing talking to Caroline. Neither one of them had a happy expression, and they were mid-conversation when I stepped out. He paused and took me in, staring at my face before slowly lowering his gaze until it hit my toes and then back up again, ending with his eyes on mine.

"Kaden convinced me that you should get fifteen more minutes of party time, and I agreed as long as you start your time at nine when I told everyone the party starts." He spoke confidently and seemed ready to walk out as soon as he was done talking by the hand he had on the door. Caroline stood there with pursed her lips, prepared to make up her argument for more time or a later starting time. She was committed to making an entrance, and the promise of an extra fifteen minutes didn't really matter, considering she had a backup plan he knew nothing about. I could see her plan of defense going across her face, knowing that when it came to Wyatt, she would win in a holdout. Her stubborn streak went far further than his.

Caroline narrowed her eyes back to him. The secret lawyer personality she held within her was aching to come out. "An extra twenty minutes, and we go out there at nine-thirty instead of nine." She threw her hand between them, allowing him to shake it in agreement.

I returned to the bathroom, not caring how they decided to proceed with their agreement, and started working on my hair. I raked a brush through the wet snarls that washing my hair had produced. Caroline had a couple of bottles of hair care products, so I picked up a bottle and sprayed it through the ends before moving on to the next one that said something about having shiny hair, which seemed like the direction I was supposed to be headed in.

Caroline came stomping into the bathroom to join me, slamming the door behind her so aggressively that the entire room rattled around us. "He acts like he owns the whole house! Why does he think he can act like that?" She let out the words and a string of insults directed at her brother that I chose to ignore. "More than anything, I want to know why I let him boss me around like that."

I slowed my movements and just listened, letting her rant without stepping in to defend Wyatt like I wanted to. I knew she wouldn't care to hear my side of the story and my agreement that we were party crashers, and as the party's host, he did have the final say over the guest list. After finishing her rant, she seemed to calm down. Caroline took a few intentional breaths, forcing her body to relax. I could tell she was starting to feel better about our situation, mainly due to her plan to sneak back in. "I am going to go shower because once I have showered, I know that I will feel better. Then we will throw your hair in Velcro rollers and give you a blowout while I curl mine."

While Caroline went to shower, I went into her bedroom and changed into something comfortable. Knowing she would take a while, I turned on the TV and found a channel that seemed to be playing old movies. Watching the couple fall in love was a good distraction, and it was funny to watch them struggle over a minor detail. If they were only willing to sit down to talk about it, then there would be no issue at all.

My phone went off with another text from Wyatt, and an overwhelming rush of emotions ran through me while I was reading his words.

Wyatt: You are so frustrating.

Felicity: What do you mean? I didn't do anything.

Wyatt's name had only three ominous dots floating beside it as he started, deleted, and then restarted another message to me before ultimately deciding not to send it, which caused my stomach to turn over with a new sense of anxiety.

Caroline came out with a new rush of enthusiasm, immediately going through her cabinets to pull out everything she would use to get us ready for the party. "Felicity, what are you doing on your phone? We need to get ready." She turned her music on, and I knew she was doing it a little louder than normal just so that Wyatt could hear it through the walls. This wasn't the first time she had used her music to make him mad, and he did the same to her by blasting his music even louder.

Two hours later, our hair was set up in rollers, our makeup was on, and a maid had ironed our dresses, leaving them hanging on the bedroom door. Caroline eagerly anticipated the arrival of party guests, frantically checking the doorbell app on her phone as people arrived. She announced each person, somehow getting even more excited each time it was someone from the upper class. Her excitement was magnified when it was someone she didn't know; somehow, that made it even more exciting, knowing that she got to make her mark on someone who didn't only know her as Wyatt's little sister.

It was a quarter to nine before she finally allowed us to get dressed, knowing that it would take a while to tie the straps of the dresses and the shoes since nothing she picked was simple.

I got dressed in the pink dress first, allowing her to zip me up tight even when it restricted my breathing. I laced up my Converse, feeling good about the stretched-out canvas material, knowing I would soon need to trade them out for the heels she bought.

Caroline tossed me some lotion and a matching perfume, which I quickly applied. It had a fruit and floral smell, which was her favorite. It was very different from the ocean smells that I gravitated to. She quickly pulled the pins from my hair and sprayed me down again with hairspray before deciding we were ready to go downstairs.

Their grand staircase had always been one of my favorite parts of their home, but tonight it felt like steps to hell, even more so as Caroline held onto my hand, pulling me down as quickly as her feet could move. Suddenly, I was even more grateful for the Converse since they were probably the only thing stopping me from landing on my face.

Loud music was bumping from the bases hidden in the walls, and it felt like the heart of the party, welcoming us inside with its rhythmic beat.

Wyatt had programmed the lights to change with the music, although they didn't allow you to see much, so I was grateful for Caroline's tight grip on me and her memory of their house.

I saw Wyatt beside the back door with Nolan and Kaden beside him. All three were dressed in simple jeans and t-shirts, probably all in designer brands, but it remained simpler than what Caroline and I were wearing.

We walked towards the boys, knowing that once we spoke to them, our timer would start, and we would only have a short amount of time to make our mark on the party. Caroline planned to soak up the party's first half by showing off who she was to everyone there. She was determined to no longer be seen as Wyatt's baby sister, and this was how she planned on doing it. The second half was when she planned on enjoying the party and her time as a redhead since she promised me no dye would touch her beautiful blond tresses until she was desperate to cover the grays.

Wyatt sized me up as I walked closer, and it caused that persistent flutter to go chasing through my body, knowing that he was looking at me in such a way. He quickly changed his expression to annoyance and spoke to his sister. "You're ready then?" His hands fluttered down to the watch on his wrist, and he started a timer, the theatrics mostly there to piss her off but also to show her that he was serious about her being on a time restraint. "Now, if you aren't back by the end of your time, the three of us will go find you."

Caroline lifted her hands and made a mocking motion to show that she heard him before pulling me along toward the game room, where most of her friends had been told to meet us. They were just as excited as she was to be here, although no one was more excited than Jessica. "Girls! You finally got down here. Now the party can start."

Jessica was the first person we saw when we walked into the room. Her electric blue dress was a contrast against the olive of her skin; it was obvious she was a little drunk, which caused a slight slurring of her words. There was no doubt in my mind she was the prettiest person in the room. It had to be how she carried herself, the confidence she had poured out of her body in waves, and probably today, it was coming out even more because of the buzz.

Caroline let go of me, pulling her in for a tight hug. Their bodies rocked back and forth in their waves of excitement. "Wyatt has us on lockdown, but I have a plan." She quickly shared her plan with Jessica, reminding her that it needed to stay on the down low if we were going to get away with it.

The drunk girl only nodded her head enthusiastically, probably unable to take in all of the details as Caroline would want her to. The other girls with her shared the excitement of being here at the party; we were all underclassmen like us and were not often invited to parties.

The girls shared their drinks with Caroline, but I opted out. It would do no good for both of us to be drunk, especially since she already had a wild plan on the agenda.

I took a non-spiked soda and sipped it graciously, nodding along to their stories as if they were as interesting as they thought they were. As different songs came on, the girls would run over to the makeshift dance floor and show off all their dance moves, cheering in surprise as if that song had been picked specifically for them.

"You don't want to dance?" His breathy whisper caused a sizzle of electricity to go up and down my spine. His chest came up against my back, and he lowered his head so his lips could dance across my ear. "I figured you weren't a big party person, but some dancing seemed like something you would do."

"It's a little hard to dance without a partner." I gestured ahead to where the girls danced in a circle, cheering each other on with their movements even as they had become sloppy with their drinking. "I can't party like they do."

His hand produced itself in front of me, only pushing his chest closer to my back, and I could feel his heat through our clothes. "Let's go dance then. I'll be your partner."

"I'm not going to go dance with you." I shook my head harder than I needed to, but I felt it was the only way to get my point across since my words always fell on deaf ears when it came to what Wyatt wanted. "I'm not a dancer. You will probably end up hurt if you try to dance with me."

His hand didn't waver, even as I disagreed with him. "Sweet Felicity." He reached for mine and laced our fingers together. "I think I will take my chances. Come dance with me."

The way our fingers became laced together caused a nervous excitement to go through me, which only grew as I saw how the other people in the room watched us.

We were a pair that no one was expecting, least of all, me.

Wyatt seemed fueled by the looks of surprise they gave as he danced his fingers down to my hips, tightening them with the promise of more to come. His lips came down again, "Flick, you have no idea the power you hold over me."

He pressed his chest against my back and got our bodies to sway with the music, and the tension was building between us each time we shifted back and forth. I could feel the tightness of his fingers on my hips while his lips fell onto my neck, and they danced there to cause a rush of goosebumps to appear up and down my spine. I was coming to realize that they would be a constant companion now that Wyatt had linked himself to me.

We kept dancing while he made a series of promises in my ear, filling my mind with thousands of ideas about the future and what that could mean for us. The original song came to an end, and as another one started, I let his hands propel my body to shift until we were face to face. His hands rose until they cradled my cheeks. "Give me a shot, Flick. We would be good together."

My head frantically shook back and forth, my eyes catching sight of a shocked Caroline as she finally started to see what was happening. Her blue eyes appeared large, her mouth was open in a state of shock, and she even seemed paler than usual.

Caroline said nothing about what she saw downstairs, instead continuing with our party plans as if nothing happened. I knew this was partially due to how much she had drunk; if she'd been all the way sober, there was no way I would have ever heard the end of it.

When Wyatt and I were done with our dance, Caroline had decided that she was done partying, at least that is what she proclaimed loudly to her brother as she dragged me back upstairs.

She pulled our disguises out and helped me change into the new dress and heels, not mentioning what she had seen downstairs. "Make sure to walk heel-toe when walking in your heels, or else you will trip."

"I'm going to pretend I didn't see any of this." Kaden stood frozen in the doorway, watching Caroline and I fluff our wigs in the mirror. "Wyatt is going to kill you if you come back downstairs."

That was what I was afraid of.

She wasn't really worried about anyone watching our return. Caroline was convinced that our disguise was foolproof, and I was choosing to have faith in her. I hoped my new look would put some distance between Wyatt and me now that the heat had been turned up.

Kaden laughed to himself as he kept walking to Wyatt's room, probably grabbing something they forgot because it wasn't long before he was walking past us again. He didn't pause; instead, he spoke over his shoulder as he passed. "I really like you as a blonde, Felicity."

Chapter 5

The Bachelorette Trip

I walked down the long row of shopping centers, searching for white and light pink clothes. The theme of Caroline's bachelorette trip was Barbie, so that was mostly what I was looking for, but I had looked so long that there was desperation in my search, and I would probably take anything at this point.

Caroline had been compared to the iconic doll her entire life, and it was a comparison she enjoyed even though she often pretended that she didn't.

Who wouldn't want to be compared to such a high peak of perfection? Especially when you were also often compared to a princess.

She was technically winning either way.

Caroline's mother, MaryAnn, had planned a series of white outfits for our weekend away that she deemed appropriate for her daughter's celebration in New York. They all looked like something Hilary Clinton would wear, which Caroline despised. Even as a teenager, she had dressed in an older fashion, often wearing something that her mother would pick and probably already owned in a more mature color.

Caroline loved to sleep over at my house in high school, especially when her dad was home, and she wanted to avoid him. She also used it as an opportunity to wear whatever she wanted. She easily fit into my mom's and my clothes, and I had fewer rules regarding the clothes that I wore.

My mom had always dressed more like a sister than she ever did a mom; our short seventeen-year age difference often meant that as I was transitioning into more adult outfits, they were the same ones my mom had worn the year before. Caroline was envious of that fact but was happy because it gave her more to choose from.

I was trying to pacify the situation, allowing Caroline to pack a bag of the clothes her mom approved of while I was bringing a second bag full of more age-appropriate clothes that she would be excited to wear for the weekend. The plan was to exchange the packing cubes so she could still come to New York with her glamorous matching monogrammed suitcases; however, they would no longer have clothing fit for a sixty-year-old.

We were trying to pull off a Trojan horse situation.

I could only imagine MaryAnn's reaction when the pictures showed what we had done. That was a problem that I wasn't going to worry about. Now that we were adults, I rarely saw Steve and Mary-Ann, so it would be Caroline getting the reaction. Thankfully, she was already preparing her apology and an excuse.

My task at the mall had me walking a thousand steps, circling the mall looking for their lingerie store without any luck. When I saw a mall employee, I rushed over to them, figuring I had walked around enough to warrant asking for help even if I didn't want to. "I am looking for Grace's Lace. Can you point me in that direction?"

They looked just barely sixteen, especially when I took in the splattering of acne across their cheeks. They pointed in the direction I had just come from with their oversized broom. "You go around this corner, and then it is on your left. They have a large white sign out front."

My cheeks flushed red with embarrassment since that wasn't the first time I had walked down that long hallway. "I'm so sorry. I must have missed it."

They stared blankly back at me, so I hurried back to where I came from, pointing my face towards the ground to cover the bright red flush that was not leaving my cheeks.

"That was hard to watch." Wyatt's tone was sarcastic and didn't make me feel better about the situation. "Really hard."

Wyatt had come with me to help but had been useless thus far. He had been busy buying soft pretzels while I searched for the store. He had perfect timing, walking upright when the teenager talked and seeing the embarrassment go through me.

My agreement to his coming was contingent on him keeping his sarcastic comments to a minimum, and his comment was crossing that line. "Shut up," I said, reaching over to push him, hoping to throw him off balance. I was shocked to find his bicep was made up of pure muscle, and my push did nothing to move him. "What are you even doing here? I thought you were getting a treat from the food court."

He lifted his large cup of pretzel bites to explain his return and shook them in my face. "I did. I got enough to share since I knew they were your favorite."

I graciously took one, shocked that he remembered these salty treats were my favorite, especially the pretzel bites from Annie's Pretzels. When we were dating, we would often stop there before our movie nights, even if we were going to be watching a movie at his house, where they had access to plenty of treats. "Yum, salty."

When I went in for more, he pulled the container away and kept it out of my reach when I desperately attempted to grab more. "Hey now, you were mean, and only nice Flick gets pretzel bites."

"If you feed me, I will be nice." I whipped out the puppy dog eyes, batting my eyelashes. It worked in the past, and I was hoping I still had enough of a hold on him that it would work again. "It's not my fault; I have a drop in blood pressure. I'm hangry, and feeding me will fix all of that."

His smirk told me he knew I was making it all up, but he returned the pretzel cup to where I could reach it. "Fine, I will share, but if your attitude doesn't change, there will be some serious ramifications."

I had no idea what that meant, but I knew him better than to argue with him when he got that devilish expression on his face.

We still hadn't gone on our date, but we had spent endless hours together, most of them with him buying us dinner and picking me up. He did not allow any of them to be called a date, stating that it could only be called a date when he picked me up and brought me something cliché like flowers or chocolate. Wyatt informed me that watching movies on the couch in my apartment didn't count as a date.

Somehow, our movie nights meant more to me than any date would have; it was like I was getting the opportunity to go back in time and get more time with the boyfriend I had loved so much.

Glancing down at my watch I realized how little time we had, and I pushed ahead now that I knew my destination, but Wyatt stopped short at the door. "Flick, I can't go in there." He whined. Wyatt gave me a wide-eyed look and gave a wild hand gesture to the sign like I was missing something. "You are going in there to buy lingerie for my little *sister!* There is no way I can go in there. That is crossing so many boundaries."

"Wyatt, I am going into this store. You can either sit out here or come inside with me." I was frustrated with his whining; he had already made a big deal about going to the mall when the new Marvel movie was available to stream. I knew that he was picking me over what he wanted to do. "Those are the two options you have."

He looked back at the benches behind us, the same ones that four other men were sitting on with their significant other's shopping bags in their hands. They all had the same flat expression, obviously bored with the mall in the same way Wyatt was. If he were to sit with them, he would only blend into the crowd.

He rolled his shoulders back and gave me a stern expression. "Okay, but you are not allowed to use her name at all. In this store, she is Voldemort. She who should not be named." Wyatt wagged a stiff finger in my face to further his point. "Am I understood?"

"Sir, yes, sir." I shot my hand to my brow and swiftly dropped it down to my side, keeping it stiff and positioned there as I walked into the store. I knew he couldn't see my eye roll, but it gave me satisfaction to do it.

I walked past the pajamas and the robes and headed toward the back, where the naughty lingerie was hidden. I could hear Wyatt trailing behind me with the slow shuffling of his feet. I wouldn't be surprised if he were doing it with his eyes closed by how he had acted at the door.

When I got to the back, I was surprised at all the white options before me. Grace's Lace was delivering on their title; many of the options were only made up of lace. "I should have grabbed a basket."

Wyatt gave a loud groan behind me. "Gross, that means you are going to buy a lot. Don't make me gag."

"I thought you weren't going to think about it." I teased him, but the look he returned showed he was not in the mood, so I continued with what I considered a helpful suggestion. "Just imagine they are baseball caps, and we are getting her ready for a big baseball game."

"Ugh, Flick!" He exclaimed, looking ready to gag by the slight green coloring overtaking his face. "That is the worst analogy ever! I do not want to think about my sister and a *big* baseball game." He exaggerated the word big with an even more aggressive, and there was a disgusted look on his face. "Gosh, have you not heard of going the bases or home runs? This was not the time for a sports metaphor."

His reaction made me giggle, and a slight blush came to my cheeks. "Okay, how about you think of them as newspapers." I tried again, racking my brain for a way he could make that one dirty. "These are *just* newspapers on the shelf. Everyone needs a newspaper, especially on their wedding night. That is a big night for reading."

Wyatt shook his head slowly in disagreement, finally choosing to look down at his feet, which was probably the safest option now that he had made this into a big deal. He popped a pretzel bite in his mouth and spoke around it, the words somewhat muffled. "The image is there, stuck in my mind forever. You might have ruined baseball for me."

"You are so dramatic. I didn't ruin baseball for you. Not that it mattered much; you barely cared about it before today." I muttered while filling my hands with some options from the shelf. There were a few times in our formative years he had stated that baseball was the most boring of sports. "You are being dramatic."

"Oh, I have always cared about baseball. You should remember that." He snickered to himself, obviously proud of being able to use the analogy against me once more.

I ignored him, instead choosing to walk around the store to look for a few more white sets to surprise Caroline. I had a handful of options in my arms when I went to him for help. He had found a wall to lean against where he worked on eating his pretzels and seemed content to play on his phone until I was done. I found a matching bra and panty set in white and her wedding colors. I held them up in front of him, clearing my throat to get his attention. "What do you think about one in their wedding color? That might be a fun surprise. Caroline might want something that isn't white. It might be nice to switch things up."

"Come on, Flick! What did I just say? She is Voldemort. We do not say her name." He shook his head in disbelief, unable to match his eyes to mine.

I didn't really want his opinion; I was only going for the reaction, and he delivered. I tried not to let him see the wide smirk across my face and walked towards the register. "Come on. After this, we can go get another treat. You deserve a reward for all of this."

He played with the perfumes on the wall and tested them against the tester strips. He was apparently keeping his back facing me on purpose. A tiny thrill went through me that I had made lingerie awkward; it made me feel better about the fact we still hadn't been on a date. He had made his intentions of asking me out known but had yet to ask me out properly. Today was technically my idea, so he couldn't even take credit for it.

Once I had the outfits in a bag and we were out the door, Wyatt finally started acting normal again. I hadn't realized how stressed he had been inside the store, but I could visibly see his shoulders relax and his jaw release tension as he calmed down. He focused on the last few pretzel bites, so I reached over to steal my fair share before he took them down. There was already half of them missing.

"Thanks for grabbing these; I was getting hungry." We had been shopping for a while, and only half of my list was crossed off. We had already decided to grab dinner once we were done, but that seemed like a lifetime away, especially at the rate we were going.

Wyatt spoke up, finally pulling his attention from his snack now that the container was empty. He pulled a napkin from his pocket for us to wipe our fingers on; I could count on him always being prepared. "What do you think about tonight for our date? I hoped we could go out before you left for the Bachelorette trip."

He was cutting it close; we left for the trip in two days. I know that he knew that since he was the one driving us to the airport, knowing him, he had to have planned that the date was tonight before this moment. He always tried to make planned things look spontaneous.

I threw my hair over my shoulder and gave him an enthusiastic smile; I hoped he could feel my excitement. "I would love to go on a date with you!"

* * *

The knock came swiftly down on the door, and my feet seemed to float me to it. I suddenly felt so light, knowing who awaited me on the other side.

On the other side of the door stood Wyatt with a large bouquet of pink roses. He presented them to me with a cautious smile on his face. "I'm hoping that these are still your favorite. After leaving the store, I realized that it might have changed in the past few years."

I took them and raised them to my nose, taking a deep breath of the floral scent I loved so much. "They are. I can't believe you remembered." I opened the door further so he could come inside my small apartment. "Let me put these in water, and then we can go on our date."

Wyatt followed me, stopping short when he reached the kitchen opening as if remembering something. He tugged on his shirt collar, indicating I had made him uncomfortable. "Well, while this isn't exactly a first date for us, I will admit that I am nervous. I keep thinking of it as if it was a first date. If we were keeping track, this would probably be closer to our hundredth date."

He wasn't wrong. This wasn't a first date for us, which was why so much of this felt familiar, even down to how he stood there with his hands in the pocket of his jeans. I remember him standing in the front room of my mom's house in the same way when I came down the stairs for our first date, with the same wide look in his eyes as if he were watching something come alive.

"Okay, so this is not a first date then. Could we simply call it a date? Take out the timeline part to fix that confusion." I proposed. The complication of it being a first date wasn't the thing that was holding me up; it was just going on a date with him. My hands quickly pulled a large glass vase from the cabinet and filled it with water from the sink. The water filled the silence that Wyatt left me with as he decided what to say next.

"That could work." Wyatt was not wasting time just standing there; instead, he walked in little circles around the room, taking everything in. He walked over to the TV and picked up some of my Knick knacks from beside it, admiring them briefly before returning them to their place. "When you said you lived above your bakery, I didn't realize you meant right above the bakery. Does it always smell like chocolate chip cookies in here?"

I could tell he was bordering on teasing and making fun of me, so I played along. "Except around Christmas, that's when it smells like gingersnaps and peppermint. That is usually when Caroline decides she needs to spend a lot of time over here, eating up all of my samples." Wyatt didn't respond; instead, he watched me as I walked back from the kitchen to the closet, grabbing my jacket and purse. The jean jacket complimented my sundress nicely. Caroline approved of it, even if she didn't know it was all to impress her brother after I had lied about it being a blind date. "Alright, hottie, are you ready?"

He nodded, choosing to stay silent when walking to the front door. He graciously held my purse while I locked the door behind me. We walked down the back steps and out of the parking lot where his old jeep sat. He had the doors off just like he did when we were teenagers; it was exactly how I liked it. There was a thrill of danger with it, even if we were just going to be riding around on the main roads. We probably would barely get to fifty miles per hour, and only if he went over the speed limit.

Wyatt held out his hand to help me into his jeep; I noted that he had kept the small step attached to the bottom. When we were in high school, he added it after I complained about having to jump up into the vehicle each morning when he picked me up. It was the first of the small surprises that he did, showing me how much he cared even when he couldn't find the words to tell me. Actions for Wyatt had always been easier, which probably had a lot to do with his parents and how their accomplishments were always displayed, but neither one was quick to express that they were proud of them.

He handed me the seatbelt, knowing it sticks on the passenger side, and I had always had a problem with it. "I must admit, because we haven't seen each other much in the last few years, you might find a few things on repeat. Since I'm low on information about you, I dug through the archives a little for things for us to do tonight. One of which was to pull the old jeep out of retirement."

"So much for being a star scholar," I muttered as he went around the back and returned to his seat. He threw his key in the engine and started to back out of the parking spot. I decided to go for a softer approach. "So, what do you have planned for this date?"

"Ah, now that is for me to know and for you to find out." He had a devilish look in his eyes. He threw his hand across the jeep and rested it on my thigh. Wyatt's fingers tapped on my kneecap with a persistent beat, probably relating to a song that was playing in his head. "Don't worry, though; I know you will like it."

I always knew when Wyatt was happy. It was how his blue eyes sparkled even as he forced his lips to remain as flat as possible. He was trying not to appear too excited, even if I knew that he was, and it made me feel better since I was doing the same. A lot was riding on this, and we both knew you rarely got such a second chance.

He drove for a while, going through parts of town that I avoided, all connected to our past in one way or another. Wyatt stretched his arm across the car, pointing out different landmarks, reminding me of moments we had gone through together. He kept driving until he reached the top of the hill, and we came to what we had always considered our spot. We would go up there after football games, taking that time together to eat whatever dinner we grabbed from a fast-food restaurant and to talk.

Wyatt was grinning so hard his face might split. "Are you ready for this?" He shouted as he ran around the back of the jeep to come help me out. His hands found mine as he helped me out. "Flick, take this as if we are ten years younger. If I had the means or the thought, this would have been our first date, not that movie on my couch."

"Hey! I happen to love our first date." I gave his shoulder a quick shove to further my point. It will always be so special to me because we transitioned from friends to more on that date. If I had known that was happening, I probably wouldn't have gone for it. "You showed that you cared about me and listened to me. That is all women are looking for."

He raised an eyebrow in my direction. "Yeah? So, can we just return to your place and talk for the rest of the night? If I had known that earlier, I would have saved myself a lot of time and money."

"Heck no, you brought me here for a date. A date that you made a lot of promises for, and I expect to be amazed." I put my hands on my hips and gave him the best serious look I could deliver, even though we both knew it was only for show. "Now come on, Romeo, make me your Juliet. Even if it must be for one night."

I walked towards the top of the hill, knowing the surprise was hidden if he kept tradition. He trailed behind me with a jump in his step, so he called out after me. "You know they both died, right?"

"Of course, I do!" I rolled my eyes in surprise. Pretending he was the expert on Shakespeare out of the two of us was laughable; he only knew the famous fated couple because of our study sessions. "I'm the one who taught you that."

He laughed, finally coming up to join me. He slid his fingers into mine and grinned widely, pointing ahead to the surprise he had waiting for me. "Come on, you are going to be late for your surprise date if we keep up this pace." Wyatt pulled me along, only stopping when my heels slowed me down. Despite his words, he wasn't annoyed with me; he seemed to like our time together no matter what we were doing. "If I had known it would take this long, I would have just driven us up here. You know they make these shoes called ballet flats, girls in the city are partial to them. You might want to give them a try."

We came up over the ridge and were overwhelmed by the light. He had strung Christmas lights from one tree to another with a large blanket beneath them, and I could see a picnic basket on the side.

"You planned a picnic!" I shouted the words as I took off for the blanket. "I can't believe you did that for me."

His laugh came out even louder than before as he followed

behind me, and within seconds, we were under the lights. They were beautiful and lit up the night sky, only adding to the bright stars. "I know you wanted to do this for my graduation, and I screwed it up by breaking up with you before then." Wyatt came closer with a bright smile on his face. "I also know I will have to keep trying to make it up to you."

"That was years ago. There is nothing that you have to make up for me."

Wyatt pulled me close by placing his hands on my hips. It was rough and primal in a way I wasn't expecting; no longer was he the sweet teenager I was partial to. "That is just a cheap excuse." He leaned down and kissed my cheek. His eyes pierced down into mine. They were filled with longing and so many deep thoughts that I could never unravel. "I screwed up once, and I will always regret that. Please know that I will make it up to you, and I promise I will never lose you again."

* * *

I stared at the clock on the dash, praying that the numbers would stop moving. Our flight took off in just over an hour, and we still had at least a fifteen-minute drive to the airport. I was nervous, but Caroline didn't seem worried, which probably had something to do with the two shots she took this morning at the house to combat her fear of flying.

It was as if we were in high school again; Caroline elected to sit beside me in the back seat with our carry-on bags in the passenger seat. It seemed planned that my seat remained right behind the driver. Wyatt used that to his advantage, staring me down each time we pulled to a stop light.

If I thought the way he held me was primal, that was nothing as territorial as his look. I tried not to let it get to me, but it was. "Wyatt, do you know that the gas is on the right? And most people hit it down when trying to get somewhere by a specific time."

"Oh, don't worry, you will be off on your little girl's trip in no time." He gave me a wink in the mirror; the light in his eyes shined. "I know you are dying to get away so you can miss me."

"What a cocky attitude you have, Mr. Calloway. Who said that I was going to miss you?" I wished I had a better response, but he was right; I would miss him. Our date was amazing; every second of it was special. He had basically transported us back in time, bringing us back to our teenage years when we would have gone to that spot and had dinner. He had planned out my favorite sandwiches, the chicken salad on croissants that their cook always made for me and fresh apple slices to dip in a warmed caramel sauce. He had even brought up a speaker to play our song, the very one he would play loudly in his car as we drove on dates and danced to at the school dances.

Wyatt wasn't wrong; we pulled up to the airport with some extra time to get through security and check in. I tried to ignore the proud smirk tied to his face as he went to the back of the jeep, pulling out our luggage so we didn't have to.

Caroline rushed out, suddenly worried about the time now that we had gotten to our destination. "Thank you for driving us!" She pulled him into a tight hug. "Try not to kill Dad while you are home, and I know I'm leaving you with Mom also, but she will be better as soon as the wedding is over. I understand if you are counting down the days; I know I am."

"As long as you are okay with it." He pulled her in once more, holding her tighter this time. I tried not to examine his muscles, but that was a losing battle. They looked so good in the short sleeves of his white T-shirt. "Be safe and have a lot of fun. You have earned a break."

It was my turn, but I didn't know how to say goodbye to him after our date. Not saying anything would be wrong considering our past; a hug seemed impersonal after our fantastic date, and it was way too early for a kiss, even if he had gone in for one last night.

He stepped forward until our bodies were flush in a tight hug. I noted that Caroline was suddenly distracted by her phone, probably by choice, so she could avoid watching us.

"Flick, I don't want you to worry about anything while you are gone. I am yours. Just remember that while I work on making you mine." He used one hand on my chin to tilt it up, making deep eye contact before gently pressing his lips against mine. I could feel the buzz of electricity between our lips. I could tell he was holding himself back from deepening the kiss as he gently bit onto my lower lip, promising so much more. Suddenly, I felt like I had found a home where our bodies connected. He was reluctant to pull away, but when he did it, I could see that it came with a devilish smile. He spoke up to Caroline, pointing in my direction. "Now you have one critical job. Take care of my girl."

Caroline gave him a mocking salute, although she was also smiling. She was very on board with the two of us getting back together and the possibility of us becoming sisters. It was the night of our date that I called her, finally admitting that Wyatt and I had something that we couldn't deny. "Yes, sir. I will ensure she has a great time."

Just as I stepped away, a swift hand came down onto my butt cheek, making my cheeks flush. I turned around to see a smirk on Wyatt's face, obviously proud of himself for getting a reaction from me. "Now go get going, beautiful girl! I don't want to hear about you missing your flight."

Caroline grabbed my arm and wrapped it up in hers. Our bags felt lighter as we plundered ahead, the excitement doing wonders for our energy. "Come on, we have a party to get to."

We hurried through the security lines and the airport, finally sitting when we got to our gate. I instantly felt better knowing we were where we were supposed to be. We were meeting the rest of the wedding party at the hotel since they were all coming from different places. Jessica was set to meet us here and had already texted Caroline that she was making her way through security after catching her own ride to the airport.

While we waited, Caroline furiously texted away, probably

sending out reminders to her fiancé, Richard, about his responsibilities for the weekend. I knew she was partially worried because he was also having his bachelor party this weekend, and all of the boys had been shockingly silent about their plans, which allowed her mind to wander and come up with a long list of fears.

Jessica came running up with a broad smile; a small blue carry-on bag trailed behind her, and as she ran, the wheels struggled to keep up. Caroline dropped her phone onto the seat beside her and swept up Jessica in a tight hug. We hadn't seen her since November at the bridal shower, even if we had all texted weekly, and you could see how excited she was to see our old friend.

She swept her bag beside ours and immediately went into business mode, pulling out her phone and reviewing our itinerary. "What is the status of our flight? We have dinner reservations and need time to refresh before we go out again. Silvia and Jen are already there, and they said that they would wait at the airport bar until we can check into the Airbnb." Jessica rattled it all out like I wasn't the one who had made all of the plans for our weekend. "Can we send them that information so they can check in without us? I know sometimes they become available early."

I pulled out my phone and completed her request, trying to ignore the twitching of my eye that came on all because she was taking over my responsibilities as the maid of honor. "Done."

The three of us were all busy women, so we filled the next fifteen minutes on our phones, clearing up any remaining business before we turned off our phones for the weekend, at least to put them on airplane mode so we could still use the cameras. That was one of Caroline's contingencies for the weekend: phones off so that we could all hang out without distractions.

The attendants called for our boarding group, and we all jumped up, collected our bags, and went to the line. Caroline couldn't stop smiling as we went towards the plane. Even the attendants took notice of her attitude; all their smiles seemed to brighten, taking her in, similar to how one would look at a newborn puppy who ran in circles around the yard without a sense of reason.

We all filed into our row, thankfully managing seats together, which probably had to do with Jessica's speaking to the man at the front desk, which produced an upgrade to each of our seats in celebration of the bride. I went in first, then Caroline, followed by Jessica in the aisle. I knew Caroline well enough to know that she had planned her middle seat with the idea of spending equal time with both of us, not wanting to look like she had a favorite.

I leaned against the window, staring out at the tracks as the rest of the plane boarded. Our kiss shouldn't have meant this much to me, but it did. I was all consumed with it, just like I had been all those years ago when he kissed me for the first time on the couch in his bedroom.

I think he knew there would be no other reason to kiss me last night unless he were serious about us, and I knew that too, which was why it scared me so much. I could brush off his words if I wanted to, but the way he held me was saying something different.

My phone buzzed with a text message from an unknown number, and while I usually would have ignored it, a feeling made me go to the message to read it, and I was not disappointed.

252-287-9230: Flick, I know you can get sick on the plane, so I slipped some gum in your purse. Chew some while you are taking off, and that should help. Order Sprite or some ginger ale from the flight attendant, and that will settle your stomach. I also added a playlist of relaxing music to your Spotify (you shouldn't still be using the passwords you used ten years ago. That is so unsafe.). It's labeled 'Wyatt and Flick,' if you download it now, it will be done before your plane takes off.

I didn't realize that his number had changed, but I quickly made the contact update on my phone and tried to ignore the thrill that went through me that he had thought to make me a playlist. My fingers flew to my Spotify, and I immediately started the download on the playlist he had created before I went to respond to his message.

Felicity: New phone who dis

Wyatt: That is not funny, and you know it.

I stared at the three blinking dots in angst, showing that he was messaging me back before I could send my next response.

Finally, after what felt like forever, his message came through.

Wyatt: It's Wyatt Calloway... sexy, funny, and the guy who knocked your socks off with the best date of your life the other night.

Felicity: I'm sorry. I still don't know who you are. I might need some more information.

Wyatt responded quickly this time, which made me feel better about how much time I had left before they came over the speakers and directed us to put our phones on airplane mode.

Wyatt: The man who you're going to dream about all week. It might help your fantasies if I remind you that I have a six-pack of abs and dreamy blue eyes, which you once told me you would swim in if you were given the chance.

Felicity: Don't you dare make me gag right here on the airplane. What sixteen-year-old girl says something like that? Even if it is to her boyfriend. That was so lame.

Wyatt: One who knew love but didn't know how to explain it. You can't call that lame; it meant the world to me. All the things you said to me mean the world to me.

The flight attendants stood in the aisle and started their speech. I knew I had only a moment or two to finish my conversation.

Felicity: Yeah, it was something like that. I need to turn my phone off. I will let you know when we land.

Wyatt: Reread my first message before you do. You can't get sick on the plane; you and I know it will stay with you for the rest of the day if you aren't careful. Make sure to listen to that playlist. It will help take your mind off the flight, and please CHEW THE GUM.

I dug in my bag for the gum, wintergreen, and my headphones. They were beside each other, so it made for an easy search.

My phone had finished downloading the playlist, so I switched to airplane mode and started with the first song. It was one of my mom's favorites from The Rolling Stones, and I could feel my mood improving with the opening notes of their instruments.

* * *

"Girlie, we have this big pool, great view, and endless drinks. Yet somehow, you can't keep your focus on anything, but your stupid phone." Caroline plopped down on the seat beside me, stretching her legs toward the pool. "What is up with you? I thought we had made a deal to leave our phones on airplane mode."

She wasn't wrong. Even though I tried, I couldn't get Wyatt out of my mind, which meant I checked my phone about every three minutes, breaking the rules and taking my phone off airplane mode. He hadn't sent me any messages throughout the weekend, even though I tried to get him to message me first by telepathically thinking about him.

Caroline didn't let me speak; she kept going with determination, unlike anything I had seen before. "So, when are we going to talk about your date with my brother? Or are you going to keep it to yourself and wallow all weekend?"

I shot up from my position in surprise, knocking my sunglasses off of my head. I could hear the clattering noise, but I ignored them, choosing instead to focus on her surprising announcement. "I thought you didn't want to know any more details. That's why I haven't said anything!"

"I know I said that I didn't want to know anything, but you are my best friend, and I only want to share in your happiness *even* if it is with my brother."

I reached across the pool chairs and grabbed her hand. "I don't want to make the situation harder on you. I know you are against this."

"It's okay, I promise. It makes sense why you lied and said it was a blind date. I will tell you that was an obvious lie. There is no way that you or Wyatt would go out with anyone else." Thankfully, Caroline still smiled and even giggled a little at this thought. This was a much different reaction than the first time she found out Wyatt and I were dating. "Neither of you are very good at keeping a secret. Not to mention there was obviously something going on when you both were busy that night or the way you just look at each other. There is some serious longing in those eyes."

"I have *not* been giving Wyatt any sort of look." I tried to keep the annoyance out of my tone, but my true feelings came through with the bitter way I said his name. "I will concede that he was giving them to me, but that is nothing I can control."

Caroline's slight giggle came out again, even though I could tell she was trying to contain it to save my pride. "Yes, you were, but the real hook and sinker was that the two of you conveniently had something going on at the same time, not to mention that you both had crappy excuses as to why we couldn't hang out." She reached over and pushed my leg, showing me that even though she was giggling, there was still a little tension beneath her words that I would be smart enough to pay attention to. "You were a better liar when we were teenagers. I expected you would have only improved with age."

Wyatt had suggested she might know something was going on after Caroline had grilled him about his plans, which he played off with the plan to go for a workout, then had to make up an excuse when she offered to go with him. Apparently, he had taken up yodeling while running to help with oxygen flow, and he advised her that it could be pretty annoying and that she would do better to work out independently.

The excuse I gave her was a little better crafted, although it apparently also fell flat based on what she was telling me. I told her that my mom and I were working on a surprise for the bride, and she couldn't see what it was yet. Thankfully, a part of that was true; we *had* prepared a surprise for her. It had just already been finished for about a month.

She gushed a little, holding my hand tightly, ready to celebrate this moment. "Now, tell me all about your date. I know I failed to be supportive the first time you did this. This time, I am your girl, a hundred percent. Spill." Caroline held a single rigid finger in front of my mouth, pausing me from saying anything despite her telling me to talk. "That is as long as we don't use any personal details about my brother because that is not something I can handle."

I quickly shared all the details of my date, not going into too much detail when it came to the goodnight kiss since she had made that boundary very clear. As I spoke, Caroline convinced me to join her in the pool, stating that was where we had our best thinking when we were younger, and it would serve us well to do it now.

"So, are you going to go out again?" Caroline floated beside me, kicking her feet onto my floaty just like she would have done in high school. It kept us close together, and I could feel the sun's heat bouncing off her skin. The white of her bikini made me first giggle when she joined me outside, the edges of it tainted with the remnants of her spray tan. "If so, I support it. I would love to have you as a sister-in-law, even if I think you could do better than my idiot brother."

I kicked up some water at her, being smart enough to avoid her shiny blonde hair. She would lose it if she had to go through the trouble of drying it for the second time today. "You have marriage on the brain. This was *just* our first date. We have no idea if it even has the potential to go anywhere."

"Is it a first date if this is your second time around? It seems more like a coming back together than a date, especially when we know how this will end." She said it like it was destined for us to be together, and we were only avoiding the inevitable.

* * *

Caroline's idea that this date had opened the door for Wyatt and me to rekindle our relationship played in repetition throughout my mind. I wanted to blame the wedding and that we were there for a bachelorette party; even the most hardened person would have thoughts of weddings and happily ever after running through their mind.

My best friend was no help; she took every opportunity to remind me of her brother and the chance for us to have our own wedding in a few months. She even volunteered to share her day with us.

I was choosing to roll my eyes and keep my attention elsewhere, knowing that speaking up to disagree would only fuel her more. Just like her brother, she enjoyed getting a reaction more than anything.

The bachelorette party was exactly what we needed; we danced until dawn with our friends and Caroline's cousins. Even Jessica let loose and had a good time, making the weekend everything Caroline had pictured.

It was the flight home that had me in knots. I had chosen to keep my phone on airplane mode for the remainder of the weekend, only pulling it out for picture taking. Caroline had turned her back on to call Richard a few times. It didn't take long for Wyatt to realize I was avoiding my phone, which is why he had called his sister and declared that he would be picking me up from the airport, stating that we only had so much time and a lot to make up for.

Caroline and Jessica were supportive, helping me do my hair and makeup before stepping onto the plane. Jessica had even gone as far as to set up a driver so that the two of them didn't have to ride with us, allowing us the alone time Wyatt was apparently looking for.

"We are starting our descent. We all want to wish you a great day and thank you for choosing us for all your travel needs." The flight attendant spoke calmly into the microphone, and a few passengers cheered in celebration. The flight had been particularly bumpy, and I could imagine I wasn't the only person happy to be back on the ground.

Once the plane stopped, the three of us stood and grabbed our carry-on bags, hurrying to meet the rest of our bags at the baggage claim. Jessica immediately pulled out her phone and started furiously texting as we walked, choosing to use Caroline and me as her eyes as we returned to the front of the airport.

"Someone seems to be excited to see you." Caroline giggled. She tapped onto my arm to bring my attention up from its position on my cell phone. I had finally decided to take it off airplane mode and the number of notifications I had received was astronomical.

She wasn't wrong. Wyatt stood beside our baggage claim with a dozen pink roses in his hands and a particularly sly smile across his face, obviously proud of himself and how he was able to go around my ignoring his messages.

I dropped my bags into her hands and took off running, not caring to slow down until I was back in his arms. My feet moved faster than my thoughts, but they all settled when he held me.

Our chests crashed together, and my hands flew to his hair, pulling him to me as closely as possible while my mouth searched out his. He had caught me in such a perfect way that my legs wrapped themself around him, pulling me against him even tighter. His small chuckle let out as he finally released my lips from his; although they didn't stray far, they planted themselves onto my neck with a playful nip. "You missed me that much?" Wyatt's hands gripped my hips in a way that drove me crazy, allowing me to feel centered as he let my feet finally rest themselves back onto the ground. "If I knew a pack of gum and a playlist would get me this type of reaction, I would have done it a lot sooner."

"You are getting this reaction because you were sweet enough to do those things to ensure I had a good time." I pressed my lips tightly against his once more, feeling at peace now that I was in his arms. "You did not have to do all of this."

I took the roses from his hand and pressed my nose into the buds. Their floral scent hit me in the face, just as it did every time he surprised me with flowers.

Caroline and Jessica joined us; in their hands was my discarded purse and carry-on bag, which Wyatt gratefully took from them. "And how are the two of you? Did you have a good trip?"

My travel companions gushed over the trip and all that we did, sharing details about the spa treatments we got to experience and the food. Jessica had been particularly excited about the restaurants and the bars. She had gone the extra mile by stalking some of them online, especially the ones who had handcrafted drinks.

All of us agreed the drinks we got there were one of a kind. There was one we all particularly enjoyed. The glass was soaked in jalapeno juices so that every sip of the drink was infused with the spice.

It was unlike anything I had ever had before, and all I could think about was sharing it with Wyatt. He would love the spicy details that were there within the drink. Not to mention the aged whiskey on their menu, something that he and his father would both go crazy for if they were given the chance to try it.

Our bags came out first on the carousel, Wyatt assisted each of us with grabbing them and helping us carry them out to where the girls' car was waiting for them. A large black SUV awaited outside, and a driver stepped out to get their bags.

"You should have seen your girl out there." Jessica was teasing him, but her eyes never left mine. The sincerity behind them made me stand taller; this past week, we had mended the friendship we once had in high school. Now that Wyatt was in the mix, I worried about how fragile that friendship was. "She is a force to be reckoned with. You would be a fool to lose her now that you have been given a second chance, and you are no fool."

A weight suddenly felt lifted off of me, allowing me to lean into Wyatt's body. His hand tightened around mine, and I felt instantly comforted by his touch, knowing that it reassured me of how I was feeling and that his touch was full of promises for later.

Chapter 6

Junior Year

Wyatt ran up the side of the field, stopping short in front of Caroline and me. The grin on his face stretched from one ear to the other, obviously happy with their win. "What did you think of that?"

"You were amazing!" I cheered for him with a wide smile across my face. Our movie night remained heavy on my mind while I waited impatiently for another moment alone with him, something that he seemed reluctant to give me.

Caroline joined in my celebration, congratulating her brother on a job well done. However, she had other things on her mind, so it came out half-heartedly. She had been eyeing the other team's tight end the entire night and was ready to make her move. "What do you say about joining their party tonight? I heard some of them talking about it."

"You want me to go to the party of the team I just beat?" Wyatt's face fell flat while his eyes ran over her face, probably convinced that she was messing with him. "I can't imagine they would want me there, *and* I don't want to be there."

Caroline only rolled her eyes back at him. She did not see that as a problem like he did. "But they would want Felicity and I there. We are hot." She had already talked my ear off about this party for the last hour, and there was no way he was going to slow her down even if he kept giving her the same unentertained expression. "I understand if you don't want to go. But can you, at the very least, drive us there? Anyone from their school probably already left, and the driver has the night off tonight."

He shifted his football pads over his shoulder and seemed to think over her proposition before swiftly shaking his head no, doing it all to get a reaction out of her. "Caroline. If you want to go to a party, you will need to find your own ride. If you are okay with coming home and hanging out there, then I have a ride for you."

"And I don't want to go to the party. I have a lot of studying to do, and Mr. Medina assigned me that essay, which I have to get through." The words flew out of my mouth as I jumped in with a lie to get out of it. I had finished all of my homework at lunch, figuring I would have to go along with whatever it was Caroline wanted for our week-end, and that would require a clear schedule. Now, all I could see was an opportunity to spend time with Wyatt. "Maybe Jessica would want to go with you?"

Within the span of my sentence, her mood had gone through some noticeable dips, ending with a bright and cheerful smile. "You could do your homework on Sunday. I won't monopolize the *entire* day with our spa plans." She tried to reason with me, but it was in vain. Caroline's mind had already moved on to making plans with Jessica; her suggestions were only out of courtesy.

"Go with Jessica. I'll be fine."

She yanked me in for a tight hug, probably feeling relieved that I was okay with her choosing Jessica over me. Of the two of us, she was the one to party with anyway. Caroline always had a hard time spending time with both of us. When she was with Jessica, she was very carefree and was apt to make poor decisions. We worked on homework and laid around in the pool when she was with me. I knew I was dull in comparison.

Caroline cheered. "Thank you! You are the best! Get Wyatt to take you home, and I will text you later."

There was a good chance I would receive more than a text; she had a penchant for phone calls when she was drunk, even if you were in the car beside her.

Caroline went running after Jessica to pull her into her party plans. I could tell how easy it was to convince her by the enthusiastic nodding of her head. Jessica was always ready to party, something I was not.

Wyatt tossed his arm across my shoulders, and I tried to ignore the stinging smell of sweat that covered his soaked pads. "So, can I assume you said no to Caroline because you wanted to spend time with me?"

I giggled. I looked up at his face and felt like I couldn't control myself around him. Once I saw he had a matching dumbstruck smile, we both seemed to enjoy the idea of some alone time. "Your assumption would be correct.

His hand drifted lower until his fingers laced with mine. I felt a flutter as our hands connected. He didn't seem to care that those around us were witnesses to it. "Let's go to my house. I want to spend time with you. Everyone's gone tonight, so we don't have to sneak you in."

That was the least of my worries, but it did make me feel better. Caroline would not be happy if she knew we were together. I was still working on telling her we had feelings for each other. "I should let my mom know where I will be so she doesn't worry." I fished in my bag for my phone while he searched in his for the keys to the jeep.

He started putting his football pads in the back while I texted her and impatiently waited for her response. As I stared at my phone, my foot stomped in a rhythmic beat against the ground. "And if she says no?" He was obviously baiting me. It was no secret that he liked bad girls, which was very far from who I was. "Then what are you going to do?"

"*Then* we will have to sneak around some more." I tried to say it casually, even though her wrath terrified me. I could only imagine her reaction if I did break the rules, which would be worse if she caught me sneaking around with a boy. Thankfully, it fell in my favor, and she responded that she was busy at work and didn't care where I would be as long as I was safe, but I wasn't going to tell him that. I liked the way he looked at me when I was the 'bad girl', and I enjoyed the thrill of being that person for him, so I lied, pretending she hadn't answered. "Looks like we are going to find out. Do you think we can keep it a secret that I'm going to your house?"

He threw our bags into the backseat and helped me into the jeep with a hand on my thigh. "I think I can manage that." I could tell he was trying to appear mischievous as he dropped his tone and stared at me through his eyebrows, deep and meaningful. "The question is if I will be able to give you back."

"You have to. Neither one of us can handle Caroline by ourselves."

He laughed as he got inside, dropping the previous exterior expression as he began the drive back to his house. Wyatt turned on some music and let the bass bump away the nerves we were both feeling. No one was home when we pulled into the garage, which made me even more nervous for what his comment about not giving me back meant. Not only were we sneaking around behind Caroline's back, no one else knew I was here.

"What if I order a couple of pizzas? When I'm done showering, it should be here." He leaped out of the jeep, coming to my side to help me. His hand was suspended in the air like a proper gentleman, something I wasn't expecting. "A meat lover special for me and then a ham and pineapple for you with green bell peppers."

"It's scary how well you know me." We had only known each other for a few short months, but he constantly surprised me with his ability to pay attention to even the smallest of details. "Really scary."

"That's only because you didn't realize I was paying attention. You aren't secretive; you're pretty open about how you feel about things, especially what makes something your favorite." He shrugged, trying to play it off like it wasn't important. His finger came up to tap my nose, emphasizing his point. "Your facial expressions give you away. The look in your eyes sometimes gives you away first, but that one is easier for you to hide from the rest of the world. It's only caught by someone watching."

"Okay, Mr. Know-it-all, what makes Hawaiian pizza my favorite?" I followed him up the steps from the garage until we were in the kitchen. Then I shifted my body, staring him down with my arms folded across my chest. He was much larger than I was, and I could do nothing if he really wanted to get past me, but thankfully, he stayed in place as if my stance was actually powerful.

It was hard to keep the smile off my face, but somehow, I managed to stay in my poker position, which only made Wyatt's grin break out enthusiastically. He liked that I was putting him to the test; most of the girls he dated would never act in such a manner. "It has fruit and two vegetables on it, so in your mind, it's basically a salad. It is the healthiest pizza."

"Two vegetables? You only said the bell peppers." I quizzed him harder, looking to see if he knew what he was saying and not just repeating the sentence I had told Caroline. "That is one vegetable. You might need to check your math."

"The sauce's main ingredient is tomatoes, which is technically a fruit, but if I say that, you will only argue that it doesn't go in a fruit salad, so it's not a fruit." He rolled his eyes down at me, knowing he had won. "Give me a harder one next time." He dropped his football gear into the mud room and gestured for me to follow him up the stairs, going deeper into his lair. "I know you and Caroline always shower after games. You can shower first, and I will give you a change of clothes. Then, you can hang out in my room while I shower."

I appreciated that he remembered that insignificant detail, even if showering in his room seemed far more personal than our current relationship.

He directed me into his room, and I got to see the mess that was missing the first time I had come over. Not so subtly, he kicked a pile of clothes into the closet and swiftly closed the door behind it, making me question the kind of mess hidden behind that door.

Out of the dresser, he produced gray Nike sweatpants and a worn t-shirt with our school logo on the front. "I'll show you how to work the water." We went into the bathroom, and he turned the shower on for me, demonstrating how to adjust it if needed. It was a pointless lesson since Caroline had the same shower, but we were both nervous, and filling the silence was the best way to go. "Just shout if you need anything." He returned to his bedroom, shouting over his shoulder as he went. "I'll be out here when you're done, and we can switch."

I took in the messy bathroom and cleared a space on the counter for his clothes, locking the door before stripping and getting into the warm water. I tried not to spend too much time in there. Still, I took my opportunity to observe the different soaps he kept in there, including the purple shampoo, which I knew Caroline convinced him to start using after noticing his blonde hair was beginning to look the shade of brass, something she was determined to avoid if possible. While she would never admit it, she agreed with her mother that each person reflected their family."

He had what looked like clean towels hanging from a rack, so I wrapped one tightly around my body and used another on my wet hair. His clothes flooded me due to their size, and they had a deep musk smell that was all Wyatt Calloway. I raised the neck to my nose and took in a deep breath full of his scent.

Whatever he was doing, it wasn't quiet as he moved around his bedroom. I could only imagine he was trying to fill the time until I joined him.

I opened the door with my cheer uniform clutched in my hand, unsure of what to do with it now that I was wearing his clothes. "I'm done. Where do you want me to set these? I left my bag in your jeep; I can grab it while you shower."

He was at my side in a flash, offering a clean sports bag with a basketball logo on the front for me to put the clothes in. Once I did, he tossed it beside his bedroom door, now in the place of a previous pile of dirty clothes that he must have cleaned up while I was in the shower. "I'll be fast, I promise. If the doorbell rings, just grab my phone and talk through the doorbell. Just tell them to leave it on the porch, and when I'm done, I will grab it." He deposited his phone into my hand and then kissed my forehead before disappearing to the bathroom to shower.

Wyatt had obviously taken my absence for the opportunity to clean up since the bedroom was cleaner than it had been before, something that only made me smile. His TV was the same model as Caroline's in her own room, so I messed with the remote until I found an older show playing a rerun episode. I used that as a distraction while I waited for him.

The temptation to snoop through his phone was strong, especially as it sat in my hands unlocked.

Caroline had been kind enough to gossip about her brother and the crush he must have on a girl in our grade. As he was a varsity football star, anything about him became hot gossip among our group of friends, and because Caroline lived with him, she always knew what was happening between him and his friends. Since his friends were teasing him about wanting to ask an underclassman out on a date, she felt this was an accurate piece to share. Only a fool would assume that he was talking about me; even as I sat in his bedroom, I knew better than to assume anything about Wyatt Calloway.

"Has the pizza not come yet? They had said fifteen to twenty minutes." Wyatt appeared behind me with his own combination of sweatpants and a worn T-shirt. His normally pale hair was darker than usual, and the water had made it into a tight curl that made him look somewhat boyish.

Grateful I had resisted the urge to snoop, I handed his phone back to him. "No, but there might be a lot of people ordering pizza tonight since it's a Friday night. I doubt we are the only teenagers on the hunt for carbs."

He jumped onto the couch, coming in close to me so that our

bodies were touching, and he stretched his arm across my shoulders, a massive difference from the last time we sat beside each other. "What are you watching?"

I explained the premise of the TV show: one guy and twelve women are all trying to end up with him. The bachelor dates each woman throughout the show, then the finale is where he proposes to the woman, and then they do a fake interview where they pronounce each other the love of their lives before the ultimate downfall that happens in six months when they break up.

"That sounds awful. Why are you wasting your time watching something like this if they are only going to break up?" Wyatt peered down at me with a raised eyebrow, his signature move that always made me want to swoon. The twitch of his lips pointed that he knew it would do something to me, and it had all been intentional. "That seems pointless."

"Remember Snoop Dogg and his wife? We all want something that makes us believe in love." I didn't get his response because his phone went off, announcing someone at the door, which had to be our pizza. He gave me a brief cheerful grin before racing off after it, obviously happy that the prospect of food was near.

* * *

"*Top Gun?* You're joking, right?" Wyatt and I had been secretly dating for three weeks now. Most of the time that consisted of movies on his couch since going into town could get us caught, especially by Caroline since she and Jessica were currently on the hunt for homecoming dresses at the mall, and that was pretty much the only cool place to hang out in our town.

I was just grateful we were together, so I didn't care that we were sitting on the couch for another night. What I was not happy with was him choosing the movie for yet another night in a row when it was my turn.

"Yes, *Top Gun.* You know you love this movie as much as I do."

He tried to reason with me, throwing in the puppy dog eyes I knew so well. Wyatt always added them in when he really wanted his way. "It would make me so happy to watch it."

"No, you're so right. I do love this movie. I *love* it when they all play football. That's when they are all shirtless on the beach. Abs, abs, and more abs." I countered, hoping that would change his mind, knowing I would only be watching the movie so I could drool over all the attractive men. "I do not love the rest of the movie. There can only be so many clichés in a two-hour time slot."

Wyatt laughed, coming in close and kissing my neck in a slobbery pucker, causing me to shriek. His hands pinched down onto my sides, where they started to tickle me. I rolled my body back and forth on the couch, desperately trying to escape his grasp. "Yeah? Maybe I should strip off my shirt and show you what I have going on. I don't mind proving to you that it's better than anything any of them have."

He didn't need to do that. I was around him and their backyard pool often enough to know he had abs just as good as Miles Teller, if not better.

"What if we pick something else? We could do a romcom, or we could always spin the wheel." Romantic comedies were my favorite movies, but they were his least favorite, often putting us in an impasse. The solution was to use an app we had downloaded on my phone. It was a wheel that spun when you tapped the middle and landed on one of the many options, declaring one of our choices to be the winner. We had each filled it with ten different movie options so that it would be fair, but somehow, his luck meant that he came off as the winner more often than I did. We had watched a lot of action movies because of this.

Wyatt pouted dramatically. He was choosing to ignore his winning streak and was probably hoping I would too. "I don't want to watch one of your girly movies. The wheel isn't nice to me."

"What do you mean by girly movies? You cried when we watched *The Notebook*." I argued back, unable to conceal the grin on my face.

He had tried to cover up the tears, but I knew the love story between Allie and Noah affected him.

He tried to play it off by distracting me. He pulled up the app on my phone and looked over the movies we had left in our wheel of choices, most of them action or romantic comedy options. "I was crying because I had just wasted two hours watching two foolish people fall in love." Wyatt's eyes rolled, still in disbelief that a love like that was possible. "You would cry too if you watched your life slowly slipping away."

Being in love with him was easy; restraining myself from telling him was hard, especially when he made me laugh like he was doing now.

"Of course, that is just your opinion. Most people consider that movie to be a classic." I tried to rationalize my love for the cliché movie, but the expression on his face told me that he was not budging.

"I would consider *Fast and Furious* a classic. Could we watch that?" He bargained. I usually would have immediately agreed that *Fast and Furious* was an excellent movie, but saying yes meant that he would win the movie night again, which was a battle I wanted to win.

I leaned over to kiss him, hoping to help sweeten the deal. "What about another run of *The Princess Bride*? A little bit of adventure and a little bit of romance."

Suddenly, he sat up, coming out of the series of thoughts he was working through. "What do you say we do something different tonight?"

"Like watch a TV show?" We had two versions of a date: watching a movie on my couch with takeout *or* watching a TV show on my couch with takeout. That was all since we were still in hiding. "We could watch a few episodes of *Friends* or The *Office*. I think they are still playing on Netflix."

He rolled his eyes until all I could see was the whites, something I saw a lot of tonight. His annoyance at my inability to comprehend his plans saw no end. "No, not to watch a TV show. I have an even better idea!" Wyatt's lips came swiftly down on mine, interrupting me from speaking out against him like I was about to do. "I've got this. You're going to love this! Meet me at my house in two hours. When you get there, ignore the house and come straight out to the gazebo."

He kissed the top of my head. Then, he was gone out the door in seconds, pulling his car out of my driveway and onto the main road. I knew he would pick up his speed as soon as he got onto the main street, just like he always did.

"Where is your Romeo going?" Mom pondered out loud, pulling my attention away from the door. She had been in the kitchen washing dishes, being close enough to chaperone without making it too obvious. She came out to see what was happening at the sound of the door closing. "Is this the part where you partake of the poison? Because that part always seemed *really* lame to me. Why is Juliet pretending Romeo is that special when he is literally just some guy?" She sauntered over to the couch and plopped her body down beside mine. I felt myself melt into the comfortable warmth she radiated. "He is just a loser wanting to have it both ways, hot girlfriend and happiness from everyone else."

Mom was not subtle in her distaste for Wyatt after finding out he was my boyfriend, and she was very against the secrets we were still hiding from Caroline. Mom appreciated the truth more than anything. I had tried to convince her that I wanted to keep it a secret, but she didn't believe me. She chose instead to assume the worst of Wyatt Calloway, and she kept that perception of our relationship even after Wyatt continued to prove her wrong.

"He said he had an idea for something new tonight, then told me to meet him at his house in two hours." I shrugged, not wanting to get my hopes up for what he had planned, even if I was excited. "He wants me to meet him at the gazebo."

Mom cocked her head to the side and narrowed her eyes. "Do you think this is when he murders you?" She shifted her hand into a fist, pretending it was a microphone while speaking in a news reporter's voice to mock me. "This is just in. The hot-shot football player has a nervous breakdown. A random girl has been found at the bottom of the lake. Could these two stories be related? The young boy's millionaire father thinks otherwise."

I shoved her hand away, which only caused her to laugh harder. Like Wyatt, my mom was enjoying the fact that she got a reaction from me. "He isn't going to kill me. Whatever made your mind go there?"

"You don't know these rich people. They always have a few skeletons in their closets. Who knows, maybe one day it might be you." She got up from the couch with a flourish and threw her hand down for me to put mine inside of it. "Now let's go get you all pretty. I want something nice to look at when I am asked to come to identify your body."

Her sarcasm made my stomach drop. Wyatt was not going to murder me, but breaking up with me was still a very real possibility that felt inevitable the longer that we stayed in the shadows. There was no way he was happy just to sit on the couch watching shows with me week after week, and his coming up with a bold new idea for tonight only pointed toward that being true.

Thankfully, Mom was having plenty of fun on her own, and she didn't seem to realize that I was worried. She dragged me up the stairs to our joint bathroom and gestured for me to sit on the closed toilet lid.

I obliged, and she immediately went to work, plugging in the curling iron and grabbing our makeup bags from the cabinet. She quickly tossed the contents into the sink so that they were easy to grab. Mom first reached for the heat protectant, spraying down my hair until it felt slightly saturated. "I say we keep it light, very innocent, and dew-kissed. He needs to think that you are naturally the most beautiful girl ever to walk the planet without effort." Mom had more skill than I did in hair and makeup, so I let her get to work, choosing to trust in the process.

She chatted away about her work while she gave me a makeover.

Mom even went as far as to turn my body away from the mirror, declaring that it wasn't a proper makeover if there was no shock factor at the end, just like they did at the end of the makeover TV shows she was so fond of.

I tried to calm my racing heart while she gave me a pair of tight jeans and a soft pink sweater to change into, grabbing my tall brown boots from behind the couch to complete the outfit.

"Now, look at your fine self." Mom turned my body by pressing on my shoulders, then held onto me while we both took in my reflection in the mirror. "You look gorgeous!"

That wasn't a word I would typically use to describe myself, but today I would accept the compliment for what it was.

I felt gorgeous.

She had curled my brown hair so that it fell in light waves down my back, using makeup to make my tan skin seem to glow, and the purple eyeliner she used made my brown eyes appear to have dramatic flakes of green in them. "You did such a good job, Mom. I don't even recognize myself."

The skinny jeans she was letting me borrow clung to my hips, making the curves work for me, and the soft pink of the sweater was delicate and feminine, just the way she wanted it to be. The entire look was better than anything I could have put together on my own, which was usually how it went.

"I figured the boots and the sweater will help you beat hypothermia while they are trying to find your body. It will give us a few extra minutes." She made one last dead daughter joke, laughing at herself while leaving for her purse and keys. "Come on now, we have a cute football player waiting for you."

The drive to the Calloway house was silent, only the radio's light tune comforting us while I contemplated if it was worth meeting him. Caroline was out at another party with Jessica, so I didn't have to worry about her being home, but both Steve and MaryAnn's cars sat in the driveway, which was unsettling. It was always a bad sign when they were both home at the same time.

Neither one of them would want Wyatt to give his energy to a girl right now, especially one that could convince him to stay here and not go away to college like they intended him to.

My body shook like a leaf as I walked around the back of the house, going through the gate and passing by the always vacant greenhouse. A ray of light came from the gazebo, and I could make out a distinctive Wyatt shape in his maroon letterman jacket leaning against one of the posts. I could only attribute that to why I kept moving towards him, despite each step feeling heavier than the one before.

He had cleared out the normal table and chairs that sat there and instead had a large mass of pillows and blankets set up facing a projection screen, already displaying the opening scene from *The Princess Bride*. He had taken the time to string white Christmas lights through the banister and then had a small picnic basket full of snacks beside a small stack of pizza boxes. I stepped inside the gazebo and twirled in a circle to take in all he had done. My hands were moist with my nerves, so I swiped them against my jeans before extending them out for him to take. "Wyatt, what is all of this?"

"Flick, you deserve a real date. I am done hiding away on your couch every weekend when we could be in the open." Wyatt took advantage of my upturned face by looking into my eyes sincerely. His hands brushed against my hair as he came in to caress my cheeks. "I love you, and I need you to know that. I need everyone to know that. No more hiding this."

I felt my knees start to grow weaker; the deeper into my eyes, he stared. The flutter behind my body caused me to fall for him more than I had initially intended. "You love me?" The words came out hesitantly. Some of me didn't believe him even though I desperately wanted to.

He pressed his thumb against my nose tenderly, pressing it in until there was a row of small wrinkles, which I knew was the whole reason he did it. This wasn't the first time he had done something like that, reminding me how much he loved my button nose. "This is true love. Come on, princess. Do you think this happens every day?"

"Quoting *The Princess Bride*, huh?" I tried to contain the overly enthusiastic grin, but it quickly overcame my face. I loved that he quoted Westly, The Dread Pirate Roberts, and he did it often. Wyatt knew how much I loved the hero of the movie and how he told Buttercup he loved her. "You're just trying to get onto my good side."

"Only when it applies." His lips pressed against my forehead, and I fell for him impossibly further. The idea of what was between us being true love felt silly but also felt right. "And it applies to a love like ours."

I tried not to giggle at him but lost that battle. His sincerity was more than I expected from the teenage boy who stood before me.

Instead of responding to him, I diverted his attention elsewhere. Bringing his face down until it is adjacent to mine, I press my lips against his. Its pressure was light, and I moved my lips against his, feeling their warmth against mine.

His hands ran their way up and down my sides until they landed on my hips. He let them stay there for a moment before letting go and breaking away from our kiss, stepping back while keeping a smile on his face.

Wyatt was a perfect gentleman, helping me move to the mass of blankets and facing me towards the movie playing on the screen before us instead of continuing the make-out session I was partial to. Somewhere behind us was the projector, and Wyatt used his phone to control it, restarting the movie and turning up the volume until it was comfortable for us to watch. Wyatt covered me with the blanket, having thought through the heavy chill in the air that floated across the water and how I would handle it, even going as far as to wrap my hands tight in his to keep them as warm as possible. He blew warm air onto them, then tucked them tightly within his own.

"So, does this count for your movie choice?" Wyatt asked, returning to our conversation from hours earlier. I knew he was saying something to fill the silence we were sitting in since that was something he struggled with, and also so we could watch *Top Gun* the next time we sat down for another movie night.

"Fine." I agreed, accepting that with his grand gesture, tonight probably meant that we wouldn't watch movies like we had been. A pang of sadness went through me, knowing that change was inevitable and I should be okay with it. It also made me realize that we were out of our safety bubble and there would be no return to it moving forward. Somehow, without either of us saying it, we knew everything had changed.

Chapter 7

Rehearsal Dinner

Caroline was ready to go, but MaryAnn was not. Thankfully, that was something we had all expected and were prepared for.

The bride's mother had taken over Caroline's bedroom. Her beauty team fluffed and fixed her hair in front of the mirror for what felt to be the millionth time, laying each of her curls down in strategic places, wanting them to fall into something resembling Hollywood waves. "We need to ensure Caroline is ready to go down the left side of the staircase so that it looks uniform when Steve and I come down. The left is my best side, so all photos need to be taken from that angle." Caroline sent me a pleading look while MaryAnn went on with what could only be considered a speech. "Has anyone figured out what side Richard has his hair parted on? If he chooses the left, then this entire thing falls apart. We need to make sure that it's on the right side."

Both sets of parents were making an announced entrance this time, and MaryAnn was very excited to be a part of it. She had already instructed all the photographers with her own list of shots. By the night's end, they would have just as many pictures of her as there were of the bride.

The bridesmaids were all dressed and waiting near the door, ready to match up with their respective groomsmen. I had tried to get ahead of this mess by requesting them to be prepared long before the party so they wouldn't be a problem when it was time for the party to start.

I should have been standing there, too, but as the maid of honor, I needed to help Caroline put the finishing touches together for her look before the party. Wearing white to all these events had seemed so exciting in the beginning, but now Caroline was getting tired of all-white outfits. This time, she opted out of the white shoes and chose bright blue Manolo Blahniks instead, just like the ones Carrie Bradshaw wore on Sex in the City.

MaryAnn protested the shoes since they were outside the wedding colors and would not fit the party's theme. Shockingly, Wyatt came to his sister's aid, fighting for her right to wear what she wanted since she had followed her mom's lead for almost a year, agreeing to every over-the-top celebration. The party was black and white, and all attendees were only allowed to wear one of the two set colors, so the shoes would only make her stand out in the crowd.

Since the bachelor and bachelorette party, Wyatt had spent most of his time in New York; just knowing he was somewhere in this house made the hair on the back of my neck stand up in anticipation. I missed him more than I should have, but he made good on his promise to fight for me even as distance made it hard. Wyatt delivered flowers to my apartment so often that I had to keep many of them in the shop, giving each table its own floral arrangement, which made many customers happy.

"Mom, you look great." Caroline had repeated that sentence enough times it had lost its weight, but that didn't stop her from saying it once more in hopes that it would calm MaryAnn down this time.

Caroline's future mother-in-law, Patrice, sat calmly on the edge of the bed, thankfully already ready. The only sign she was frustrated was when she would impatiently check her watch, glancing with her eyes down every five minutes to see how close we were to the party. She was probably checking to see how close she was to escaping this room.

Patrice was not one for parties like this. She had made it clear to us all in the first wedding planning meeting that she would show up when needed, but otherwise, her only contribution would be financial. She owned her own pharmaceutical company, Grinolds, and most of her energy was put towards that.

MaryAnn finally felt comfortable with her outfit and the way her bleached blonde hair was lying, and she moved away from the mirror. She immediately returned to barking orders to the bridesmaids like they were her personal servants, not losing steam despite how close we were to the start of the party. "Will someone go get the groomsmen to stand at the top of the stairs? We also need the fathers and the groom ready. I just know Steve probably convinced Jim to smoke a cigar in his office, so someone will need to go get him."

I sent Caroline an apologetic look and raced for the door, wanting to be the one for that job since it would give me an excuse to leave the room and get out of Caroline's way. A smart person to send would have been Jessica; she knew the house as well as I did and also knew who MaryAnn wanted checked on. She also didn't have the job of directing the group. "I will go make sure they are ready. I will be back before we need to go downstairs." I could not get out of the door fast enough.

Once on the other side, I knew I could finally take a deep breath. I only heard the door close behind me when my body slammed into a wall of solid muscle.

Wyatt's smirk showed how great of a situation he thought this was. His hands closed around me, keeping me from falling to the ground. His hands came down onto my hips, his favorite resting place. "What are you doing out here?"

His suit had been pressed to perfection, and his blonde waves had been gelled until the normal mess of curls looked tamed in a way, I wasn't fond of. I preferred it when he looked unruly. The less put together he appeared, the more he looked like the version of Wyatt my heart considered mine.

He only wore his hair like that when he played a part for Steve and MaryAnn, trying to appear as perfect as possible as if it was required for the position. Caroline did the same thing, choosing to wear respectable colors and tones because she knew they favored that. The worst was when she would wear those pantsuits her mother loved so much, even though they made her uncomfortable.

His blue eyes sparkled with a boyish mischief that I knew too well. "I was coming to see you." Wyatt's arms came around me, and he pressed himself into me until I was backed against the wall. His movements were fast and smooth, making me wonder if this was a move he had practiced. His lips enveloped mine, taking a second to nibble to get a gasp of surprise out of me, which only caused him to tighten his fingers against my hips even more. "It's been too long since I got to do that."

I felt the same way and happily leaned into it and kissed him again. I had forgotten how good it was to kiss him, but this reminded me why our studying dates in high school turned quickly into an excuse to make out. "It has been too long. We need to make sure to kiss at least once a week." I tried to sound serious, but that was hard when his hot breath was coming down the sides of my neck. The sensation caused a rush of goosebumps down my sides and a sharp intake of breath. "If we go this long without, I start to go through withdrawals."

"Oh, more than that. I am requesting we kiss at least once a day. Maybe even once an hour if I allow myself to be a tyrant like I want to be." He bargained, not letting up from his position against my collarbone. Even though I could tell he was trying to be funny, his words showed some real sincerity. "You think you are going through withdrawals; I was withering away without them. It's like I am a man released from prison, finally getting to experience the sun on my face and the rush of freedom through my hair."

I scrunched my nose, trying to contain the eruption of emotions he was creating with his vulnerability. "You are being so dramatic." I stayed in his arms for a second longer, soaking in the feeling of him being near before I remembered the tasks that had allowed me to escape the bride's room. I pushed against his chest and shook myself free from the cage he had put me in, physically *and* mentally. "How do you feel the rush of freedom through your hair when it is gelled down so thick? You look plastic. You look like a Ken doll."

He rolled his eyes dramatically to get me to laugh, lightening the energy mostly to show me he wasn't offended at my pulling away. "I am at least a G.I. Joe doll. I am rugged and tough. Check out these muscles." He flexed his left bicep close to my face, displaying the muscle even through the tightness of his shirt. "Aren't they G.I. Joe worthy?"

"Not with those blonde curls and this suit. You are all Ken." Remembering my original task, I took another step away from him, bringing my focus back to life since he had the skill of making me lose my attention, especially when he flirted with me. "She's ready. We have to get this going."

"Do you mean Caroline is ready? Or is it that my mom is finally ready? Because those are two very different things." He rolled his eyes, no stranger to the timetable of the Calloway Women. "Your answer will also determine how close we are to this party starting. There could be an hour difference in those answers."

"All I'm going to say is that the women are ready. I have to ask if you wouldn't mind gathering the groom and the rest of the groomsmen while I find the fathers?" I tried to soften my face and added the slightest pout, hoping it would persuade him. If he took that one job off of my plate, then we might actually pull this off and get everyone downstairs in time. "Please? You would be doing me a tremendous favor."

He came in with his negotiation even though I knew he would do it for me regardless of my answer. "Only if you kiss me one more time. And it has to be a good kiss with lots of passion to make it last the hours until we get to do it again."

Happily, I obliged his cheeky request by pressing a quick peck to his lips before pressing my hands against his chest and shoving him toward the groomsmen, allowing the kiss to hopefully only be full of the promise of more. "Now go! The party is about to start without us."

Wyatt went, and I only paused a moment to watch the way his butt looked in his black slacks before reminding myself of my goal, taking off down the back servant's staircase towards Steve's office. The fathers had held themselves up for the pre-party festivities, choosing to smoke their Cuban cigars and drink their scotch away from the rest of us.

The staircase had been without use for a long time, and I mindfully stepped around the spiderwebs, trying to avoid getting dirt on my dress or my skin. MaryAnn would lose her mind, knowing that I chose to find the fathers by taking this path and not the traditional route. At the bottom of the staircase, I let my hands pause on the handle, taking in the sounds hidden behind the door so I could best know when to sneak through. I tried to make my movements as smooth as possible as I opened the gap between the door and the wall, slipping my body through the crack and seamlessly joining the movements of the kitchen.

Emsley had the entire kitchen staff running in circles, preparing for tonight like soldiers getting ready for the Calloway war. MaryAnn could only handle excellence, and Steve being home added to the pressure. He would not hesitate to kick someone off of his payroll.

I gave a nod to Emsley, taking in her bright red hair and the frazzled look in her eyes, showing how intense the undertaking of this party was for her.

Leaving her to work on dinner, I moved forward with my task, cutting across the house and trying to avoid my mother's eye. I knew that if she saw me, it would be inevitable she would ask me for help with something. Walking up to the study, I gave the door a soft knock and patiently waited for their response. Steve's ominous voice came out loud and clear, as if he was expecting me. "Come in."

Just as I suspected, the two fathers were sitting in the office, their butts firmly placed in matching armchairs. Both of them had a cigar in one hand and cups half full of scotch in the other.

The thing that matched the most was the scowls permanently fixed on their faces. Neither of them was particularly unpleasant; they chose their moments of joy sparingly and were usually welcoming when you came face to face with them. It was apparent the two men were both done with all of these wedding festivities.

"MaryAnn wants both of you upstairs so that everyone can be ready for the party to start." My watch said that we had fifteen minutes before the party's official start, but no one was on time in a crowd like theirs. Most arrived at a party such as this one at least ten minutes late, and no one wanted to be the first person there if they could help it. "She needs you both ready for the grand entrance."

There was a simultaneous rolling of their eyes, but neither argued with me. I did notice that both of them stole a second to shoot back the rest of their drinks, both gentlemen deciding that there would be no way for them to get through this without being a little buzzed, so they both downed the last of their glasses. I could only imagine how expensive that was.

Steve presented a crystal ashtray for his partner to put out his cigar and patiently waited for him to do so. Both men stood and gathered their things, spraying themselves down with a fabric refresher to cover up the lingering smells of their indulgences.

Steve left the ashtray and the empty whiskey glasses on the coffee table, not bothering to put them away when he paid people to do it for him, which was a bad habit that I was grateful Wyatt didn't adopt. He led Richard's father to the door where I still stood. "Well, MaryAnn is probably going crazy. We best relieve the children from her wrath." Steve let out a lighthearted chuckle that was incredibly forced, all for the benefit of our company and not the way he really felt. "I have been married long enough to know better than to keep her waiting. Happy wife, happy life. If you know what I mean."

I had never heard anything so fake in my life.

I was of the theory that Steve Caloway was still only with MaryAnn because it was cheaper to be married to her than to pay her alimony, and the way he danced circles around her proved that.

Richard's father chose not to respond; instead, he silently followed Steve as he led us back to the bedrooms where MaryAnn and Patrice were waiting for them. Both of them let a mindless conversation about golf fill their walk, so I opted out of following them and instead walked back to the kitchen. Emsley appeared to have better control of her sinking ship as the wait staff walked around with choreographed movements instead of the confusing pattern they were doing before.

"You're back. Wanting to sneak back up like you used to?" Her chuckle was layered with her memories of catching Wyatt and me going up the staircase I had previously come down.

She was an in-house chef, so she had a bedroom and bathroom on the property, which was a huge reason why she would catch Wyatt and me so late at night when we failed to be quiet when coming through the kitchen. She knew we were seeing each other as teenagers before anyone else.

I quickly shook my head, reaching out to the fruit basket on the counter to grab a banana, knowing that I had not eaten all day and that even though we were eating in an hour, I would feel better having something in my stomach. "I had the option of sneaking up the staircase and risking getting dirty or walking up the main staircase with Steve. I decided to choose option three by hanging out here for a second and letting there be some space between us." Then, I would sneak back up the stairs in just enough time to avoid MaryAnn's wrath without having to awkwardly converse with Steve. "MaryAnn has been a lot to handle lately, and it seems only to be getting worse. I needed a second to breathe without her hovering."

"And in doing so, you are leaving Miss Caroline to deal with her alone?" Her eyebrow raised further to display her disappointment.

Instead of eating the banana normally, I pulled it apart piece by piece and slowly ate it, mostly hoping to find a way to get out of the conversation I brought myself into. Then fate seemed to be working against me because my mom walked into the kitchen right then. Now, I would have to justify my choices to my mother too.

I could hear a maid opening the front door, inviting a few guests to enter, and follow her to the ballroom, where tables lined up for the rehearsal dinner. By the sounds of their footsteps, it seemed like a large group had entered, which only propelled my need to go upstairs and join the rest of the wedding party.

"What are you doing down here? Caroline needs you." Mom had a lovely black dress on and a matching clipboard in her hands. She had an air of authority around her, which only became stronger by narrowing her eyes in my direction in a way only a mother could do. Her gaze dropped to my hands, and the banana sat half-eaten, which disappointed her further. "Why are you eating? I have put together an entire dinner that starts in less than an hour."

"I almost passed out the last time we did one of these. I figured it would be better for me to eat something than to risk that again." It seemed worthy of a reason to eat now, but by the look on her face, I could see that she disagreed.

She gestured to the hidden staircase behind me, knowing that would be my preferred way of returning upstairs now that guests had arrived. "Go take care of the bride."

I shoved the remainder of my banana in my mouth, handing her the peel with a regretful smile. Thankfully, the wall behind me only needed a slight push before I was able to open it up, paving a secret path to the bedrooms.

Mom quickly closed the door behind me, having the foresight to see that it would not be a good thing for any of the temporary staff to know it was there. Sadly, that forced me into complete darkness, and only my memory of the path getting me back upstairs. I pressed my hand against the cobblestone of the wall and used that as my guide.

Reaching the top of the stairs quickly, my hands fumbled across the door as I searched for the knob. Only a tiny sliver of light outlined the door, making the search a little easier.

Wyatt's voice stood out on the other side of the door, so despite my hand grasping the knob, I didn't turn it. "Where is Felicity? I thought she went downstairs to find you."

Steve's response came quickly, the snark behind his words showing how annoyed he was with the endless wedding affair and my part in it. "That silly girl probably got distracted by something. It wouldn't be the first time her youthful wills got in her way."

Steve's voice was trying to sound carefree and casual, but his annoyance at my absences showed through. Only Wyatt and Caroline would have been listening for it. The tone of his voice was clueing them when he had reached his max. I knew from experience that they both monitored their father and his tone to get an insight into how he felt.

In the normal way that narcissists work, Steve would remain cool, calm, and collected because there were witnesses. Only after everyone had left would he take out his anger on MaryAnn or the kids.

I had witnessed enough times to know that he would never hit any of them; despite how angry he would become, that was one line he would never cross.

When we were younger, Caroline and I snuck down the back staircase on our way to the kitchen, hoping to make some popcorn after everyone had gone to sleep. Steve Calloway was in the kitchen with his friends. They were in the middle of their poker night, and the normal staff had been sent home for the day, so they had to search for their own snacks after having worked through the ones Emerly had sat out for them.

Steve's voice spoke quietly to his friends, none of them wanting to risk waking up the rest of the house and disrupting their party. "She makes me so mad. She seems to think that there is an endless amount of money." He laughed, but it was controlled and all for show. He had played this dance before; putting on a show for those in his circle was nothing new. "There have been so many times that I wished I could teach her a lesson. Get her to understand what the value of all of this means."

Caroline and I stood frozen at the foot of the stairs, taking in everything they said and even more what they weren't saying since there seemed to be a heavy weight beneath their interaction. None of the other men ever said the words, but we both knew they were talking about more than freezing the money. These men were talking about hitting their wives.

Neither one of us had ever spoken about that day and what we had heard; we both had waited for them to leave before we turned around and walked back up the stairs, completely forgetting that we had been on a hunt for a snack.

I took a deep breath, shaking off the memories of that night and our past, before opening the door and sneaking behind the line of groomsmen, quietly closing the heavy door behind me.

Wyatt was the first to see me hiding behind the two large groomsmen in their dark tuxes. He had been looking for me, obvious by how his head seemed to be surveying the room, and when his eyes locked onto mine, a smile danced across his lips. It was no secret he knew where I had come from by the way his eyes sparkled; the mischief of his youth was there before my eyes.

"There she is," He remarked very casually in the same way his dad had done, knowing that the way they came off said a lot more than their words. "She is just a little shorter than the rest of our group. Easy for your eyes to pass over her."

Steven had the grace to appear embarrassed for what he said, although it didn't last long. "Wonderful, now we can get this party started."

MaryAnn was walking around the room, fixing each of the groomsmen's ties and jackets until they all sat perfectly straight.

There seemed to be an even split down the room where she had already adjusted their attire. "Wyatt, go join her for the stair walk. Your heights will be disproportionate, but it will have to do since Brett can't be here tonight."

Brett was the Best Man, so his being stuck out of town for the night left me without my walking partner. Wyatt had been temporarily upgraded, and one of the groom's younger cousins had been asked to step into the line for the night so that no one would miss a partner—just another example of how the people in their world were so easily replaceable.

Wyatt did as directed and slipped in beside me; his head came down so that his lips were pressed against my ear so that he could whisper. "Sneaking around walls again, Flick? Shame on you to do such a thing without me." His smirk did more than his words as his hand reached out to brush some dirt off my arm that I had apparently gotten when I tried to listen against the door. "Don't pretend you've forgotten it is best as a partner activity. I can't believe you went back there without me."

I bumped my hip against his and tried to give him my brightest and hopefully my most innocent smile. "I figured you would think yourself too old to get lost behind the walls with me."

Wyatt's eyes narrowed with some depth, only slightly trying to intimidate me now that he was getting the opportunity. I knew that whatever he said would stay with me forever, no matter how this weekend ended. "I will never be too old to run around with you. It would be a joy to get lost with you, Flick."

I tried to keep the grin off my face, but it remained in place. "Well, that's good to know."

Slipping my arm through his was so natural as we fell in line. We would be walking down the stairs right before Caroline and Richard with half a dozen bridesmaids and groomsmen before us. MaryAnn and Steve were at the front of the line, with Richard's parents standing behind them.

My mom stood at the bottom of the stairs with a microphone. She was set to be the night's announcer, something I was grateful for since that was typically my job. "The bride and groom are so grateful to have you join us tonight. It is my honor and privilege to present the bride's and groom's parents to you." Mom started her introductions with a large smile on her face, happy to be in charge of the event she had been hired to plan. Now that MaryAnn was in front of all of her guests, there was little she could do about my mom's decisions.

She continued her introductions with the same big and bright smile until we were all at the bottom of the stairs. I expected Wyatt to release me, but a small part of me was grateful he did the opposite. He almost seemed to hold me closer, moving his arm around my body so that his hand was cradling my hip, walking me around the party while he spoke to the guests.

Even a blind man would put us together as a couple, which seemed to be his plan because of the way he kept me close. It didn't matter that I had met most of these people before. He made a big deal by introducing me to those he spoke to, slipping into the conversation that I owned my own bakery, that it had supplied all of the sweets they would be eating tonight, and that my services were available.

By the end of our first lap around the room, I had a handful of business cards tucked into the pocket of Wyatt's tuxedo pants from all of the contacts who wanted to work with my bakery in the future.

"These are some great prospects. You might never have a free moment again. I should have thought this through: when will I ever get a moment alone with you again?" He walked us over to the side of the room, his gentle hand in mine to lead me. My heels kept me only a few inches underneath his shoulders, and they were starting to hurt my feet. There was a series of tables around the room for the older guests to sit down at. Wyatt suggested we take advantage of them, and like a gentleman, he pulled out my chair.

I suppressed my laughter and gratefully took a seat. Most of the women were very polite in their desire to employ me, but he and I knew that only one or two would call me, especially for an event that would take my time away from him. I rarely got to see him, which had nothing to do with my schedule since he was still spending more than half of his time in New York.

"It might be up to you to employ me. It would really help to put my name out there." I sweetened my words with a smile on my face. "Are you looking for a personal pastry chef? That would really boost office morale."

He leaned in and whispered in my ear so the other guests at the table wouldn't hear. Each time Wyatt's lips grazed my ear, it made my toes curl, which was probably why it was his favorite move. "Are you offering to come to my house accompanied by whipped cream? Oh, Flick, please say you have a uniform. I would die a happy man with that knowledge."

His laugh confirmed the rush of blood to my cheeks. "No, I was offering to cater a party for you, ensuring that your guests don't drop their blood sugar dramatically. That would be terrible." I pushed him back into his seat and surveyed the rest of the table guests, feeling better when they were in the middle of their conversations and were not hearing ours. "Yes, I have a uniform. No, you are never going to see it."

Wyatt threw his hand to his chest and gripped the fabric dramatically. "Be still, my heart!"

Now, that brought attention from the other members of our linen-lined table, most of them giving us a once-over glance before returning to their own conversations.

Caroline and Richard were joined at the hip and were doing their own circle around the room in the same way we had done; only for them was Richard doing his networking. While Wyatt and I mostly spoke to the female guests, the groom was making his way through to discuss with all of his father's business partners. By Caroline's bored expression, I could tell that their conversations were primarily about how he could continue his rise in the company.

She had already sold her soul to be a partner's wife, set to live forever, standing beside Richard with a painted smile on her face and a tight grip on her martini glass. From across the room, I could see Steven and MaryAnn standing in a mirrored pose.

I could see Caroline's future even if she couldn't.

The staff that my mom had hired made their way around the room with trays full of champagne glasses. They walked the room so that the guests could each grab one as they desired, and when the waiter came past us Wyatt grabbed two. He pressed it into my hand and motioned me to drink. "This will help ease the pain of your heels."

I threw back the glass in an unladylike fashion and felt the alcoholic warmth as it made its way down my throat. Instantly, my nose scrunched in a tight grimace, which made him chuckle at my expense. "I was hoping it would go down smoother," I explained, although that only caused him to find more humor in my actions. "Something this expensive should go down easier."

He reached up to scratch his jaw. He was using that to cover the fact he was actively laughing at me, but I could still see it from the slight sparkle in his eyes. "Do you remember the first time you drank?" Wyatt's face only seemed to light up more as he recalled the painful memory of that high school night when Caroline and I snuck back into his party after he had given us a party curfew. "Other than it being a very epic party."

My nod came slowly, trying to gauge where he was going before I bound myself to the memories he had of that night. Obviously, he knew we snuck back into the party, but by then, we were all drunk, so it was unknown how much of that night stayed with him.

"You were a source of light for me that night. I can admit that was just a small part of who you were to me during those years, and I don't think you always realized that. Did you know that I have attributed that very night to why I have never become an alcoholic?" He wasn't looking at me any longer; instead, he focused on the chandler above our heads. It looked like the same crystal that the champagne glasses were made from, and hidden between some of the details was Steve Calloway's business emblem. It was painted in the strings of glass beads, matching the logo displayed on the shot glasses from the very night he was recalling. It seemed as though every moment was all being connected by an invisible string.

I tried to think back to that night, trying to find a moment that wasn't fuzzy. Sadly, it had all gotten muddled together especially there at the end. "I had a lot to drink that night. I can't imagine I said anything inspiring."

Wyatt's laugh was very similar to Steve's. They cover up their true feelings with a small laugh to relieve the tension. I watched the way Wyatt desperately kept a light look in his eyes, even though this seemed to be a heavy topic for both of us. "You aren't wrong there. That is probably why I feel this way." His hand enveloped mine, and all I felt was his warmth. "Flick, that was the scariest night of my life. All I could think about was if I lost you because I was the idiot who threw a party and was too drunk to take the girl he loved to the hospital when she needed me to."

His fingers danced across the scar I had on my wrist. It was the smallest one I was left with and served as the highest reminder of the freak accident I experienced here at the Calloway house.

"It wasn't your fault." Those were probably the words I said most that night, and even saying hem now they felt just as empty. He beat himself up that night, not able to overcome the fact that it was all an accident out of his control. Gently I moved his hand so that it was holding mine and not inspecting it as I tried to reassure him. "Nothing from that night was your fault. Everything from that night is a little fuzzy, but I know that part to be true."

There was little that I remembered from that night. There was too much that was happening at once, and while adrenaline did a lot to sharpen some senses, it also had the talent of doing the opposite to shield us from the pain. I was trying too hard to focus on my breathing and on the blood that I was losing, that I ignored most of what was going on around me.

Wyatt didn't let up, obviously feeling overwhelmed by the memories, evident by the welling of tears in his eyes. Ignoring my words, he pressed his lips against the scar lightly as if he were afraid of hurting me. "Flick, I don't think you understand how I felt that night. Everything flashed before my eyes, and losing you was so close to being a reality it scared me." His eyes met mine with an unmatched intensity.

"So you broke up with me? Deciding to lose me on your own terms seemed better than staying with me?" His call to me was only about a minute long, just long enough for him to ask how I was doing and then to break up with me. There were a few extra seconds where my crying began before he officially hung up the phone, and I was forced to listen to the empty dial tone stretch on for what felt like hours. "That seems like a crappy solution to such a small problem. It was a couple of stitches and a small surgery, nothing that anyone needed to worry about."

He shook his head, obviously still wanting to discuss an old memory that would be better off staying in the past. Caroline and I had barely addressed that day, and that was on my terms. I had firmly put that day into the past. "Flick, I was doing what I had to do to protect my heart. If we had continued seeing each other and you had even gotten a papercut, it would have been my undoing. It was easier to love you from afar and to keep up with you through Caroline. If I were any closer, it would have ruined me."

"And why are you allowing yourself to be close to me now?" I had wondered about that for a while but was afraid of asking him, fearing he would run the other way again.

He wiped the tears from his eyes and sipped from his glass to stall and avoid going any deeper into the emotions he was struggling to come face to face with. "I decided that staying away from you was worse for me than it had ever been for you. I just couldn't stay away any longer."

"And you just decided I would be okay with it?" As quietly as possible, I argued under my breath, the venom behind my words carrying most of how I felt without needing volume. "That was such a crappy thing to do to me, and you knew it. Then you hid yourself away the rest of the year."

He nodded slowly in agreement, stealing another opportunity to sip from his glass. His eyebrows almost seemed to twitch along with his thoughts. "I didn't know what to do. This is why I am taking every opportunity to make it up to you while I still can."

We could keep discussing this topic, and I could try to get more information about that decision, but it seemed futile to bring up the past when we were here celebrating the beginning of Caroline's new life.

I took a few calming breaths, trying to lose the frustration and anger from that night, and after a second, I reached my hand out for him and gestured towards the dance floor where a few of the older guests were dancing to the low music of the live band. "Let us just be strangers tonight. We can pretend we met because we were close to the bride and groom. Conveniently, we were partnered to walk down the aisle, and a strange connection just came over us, and we were powerless against it."

Wyatt chuckled but was willing to go along with my wild idea. "Okay, I can do that." He stood and went to shake my hand like we were the strangers I wanted us to be. "You said your name was Felisha?"

A giggle slipped from my lips that I tried quickly to contain. "It's Felicity, and you said yours was Wyatt? What a strange name, is it French?"

"Actually, English. It means strong and brave." He subtly flexed a muscle for my eyes, making a big dramatic show. "Fitting, don't you think?"

"Why Mr. Calloway, I don't know you, but that seems like a big question. At the end of the night, I might be able to judge whether your name is fitting or not. Just as you might be able to tell me if I am fitting of mine, which is happiness, by the way."

He let me continue my game as we walked towards the dance floor. Wyatt did slip up our act as strangers when he pulled me close to him and immediately planted his hands on my hips like he had done hundreds of times before. I let myself fall into him as he swayed our bodies to the rhythm, never allowing our bodies to separate for more than a second as he released me to spin along with the music.

"So, Felicity, what brought you to this party tonight?" He questioned me like we were truly the strangers we were pretending to be.

"I have been friends with the bride for a long time. Have you met her? I believe you said that you were close to the groom." I tried to push him to see how well he could play the game. He picked up our movements to match the music's tempo, his hands never leaving my hips.

Wyatt pursed his lips as if he really had to think of the bride and where he might have met her. "I think so. Blonde hair, blue eyes, and a big nose. Right? Or was that just another one of the bridesmaids?"

The unladylike chuckle erupted from my lips, which I quickly threw my hand up to muffle. "She does not have a big nose." I slapped my hand against his chest, mostly out of disappointment for his childish humor. "Don't be so mean to your sister."

"It would only be mean if she heard me."

I pulled away just far enough from his body to look him in the eye. "Yes, and as much fun as this game is, it's who defends your name when you're not even in the room." I chastised him. "Now, say something nice about her to make up for it. We have to even out your karma."

He pulled me back against his body. "I think my karma is doing just fine. I have a gorgeous woman in my arms who wants to dance with me. That sounds like I am doing something right in the world." He must have felt by the tense position of my body that it wasn't what I was looking for because he kept going. "My sister is the most beautiful woman in this room, second only to you. You have no idea how lucky I feel to be right here with you."

I tried to hide the blush that overcame my cheeks by resting my head against him, where I could hear the steady rhythm of his heart, allowing that to be the beat we danced to.

Chapter 8

Junior Year

The lights around me flashed brilliant shades of red and blue. Each time they changed, my body struggled to adjust, and they only made the headache grow stronger.

My eyes felt heavy, but a small voice went in a nagging repetition through my mind in an insistent warning. "Don't *you dare close your eyes. You might not open them back up if you close them.*"

The voice wasn't familiar, but I let my attention focus on it since it was the only thing holding me together. The pain coming from my leg was pulsing, and the cold temperature of my drying blood caused a chill to come over me.

Wyatt's blurry figure appeared before my weak eyes. He had a frantic expression on his face that matched the intensity of the flashing police lights. "Flick. Look at me! Don't stop looking at me." His face blurred in and out of my vision, with the police lights casting shadows across his expressions. "I need you to focus on my face."

The last time he spoke, I remembered that the words had come out with a slur, but even in my foggy state, I could register that what he was saying was steady now. I could also see that he had a slit up by his hairline where he had somehow been cut, if the bright red blood was anything to go off of.

"Wyatt." My mouth opened again as I tried to say anything more than his name, but it felt too dry to get anything out. I moved my tongue around, trying to moisten my mouth with it, but it was just as dry.

"Just don't let go of my hand." Wyatt kissed my bloodied knuckles with shaky movements. A single tear came down his cheek, something I had never seen before. "Flick, you need to keep your eyes open for me."

Caroline and Jessica scurried around us, trying to get the other guests out of the way so they could come with us to the hospital. They were following Wyatt and me as the paramedics pushed me towards the door on the ambulance's stretcher. From a distance, I could hear Jessica telling Nolan and Kaden they were in charge of the house and to join us at the hospital after everyone had left.

The female paramedic on the opposite side of Wyatt put an oxygen mask over my face. Immediately, I felt the rush of pressured air invading my lungs, igniting the pain from my fall. I just knew without looking down that I was going to be covered in bruises. "Is there someone here who could call her parents?"

Caroline volunteered to make that call; she was probably the best person for the job, considering she had been the other mostly sober person in our bunch. Even without looking at her, I could hear the sound of her calling my mom, informing her of my accident and our rush to the hospital. I could also hear my mom's frantic yelling on the other end of the phone, especially since she had no idea the party was happening that night.

"How much did she have to drink?" The paramedic interrogated my friends with a stern expression. "We need to know how much alcohol she has in her system. What medical conditions does she have? Is there a risk of seizures?"

Wyatt assessed me with a scrutinizing eye as if he would see something the paramedic wasn't. "Nothing, she didn't have anything to drink but soda. She does have asthma. I can find her inhaler upstairs if you need it."

I could hear the paramedic reassure him that it would not be needed, but the information was helpful, and he would need to repeat it to the doctors when we arrived at the hospital. The entire team pushed the stretcher outside, and the cold air hit, causing goosebumps to overcome my body. Wyatt ran his hand up and down my arm to combat them as my teeth chattered out their own rhythmic tune.

My body got tipped as they raised me into the ambulance. Not leaving my side or letting go of my hand, Wyatt slid into the seat beside me and started to assure me everything would be fine. "Jessica and Caroline are coming in Jessica's car, and your mom is going to meet us there. Everything is going to be okay."

The paramedic came on the other side of me and immediately started hooking me up to different machines and even attached an IV to my arm. "We are going to start you on some fluids. They will probably make you colder, so I will place a blanket over your legs to combat it. Let me know if it gets to the point where it is unmanageable. That can be a sign that you are going into shock, which needs to be addressed." She went over her actions before doing them as if I were in a state of awareness where I might react. I wasn't even fully aware if moving my head was possible with the neck brace they had put on me as soon as they arrived at the scene, just seconds before they shifted me onto the stretcher and started to administer care. She directed her attention to Wyatt and started giving him directions. "Please keep an eye out for this as well. If you see a change in her coloring, tell me about it immediately."

There was very little chance that his attention would waver from my face, and that reassured me that very little would change without his knowledge. I felt safe having him there with me.

My eyes became heavy again, and I fought to keep them open. I could feel Wyatt's hand on my shoulder, shaking my body, trying to keep my attention on him and my eyes open. At the same time, he screamed for me to stay awake; the paramedic leaned over me with an intense look across her face while yelling at the driver to move faster, and then suddenly, everything went dark.

* * *

"Where is my baby?" Mom's emotional voice broke through the darkness, which I continued slipping in and out whenever someone new entered the room. "I need the room of Felicity Abbott! I am her mother. Where is she?"

Jessica had offered to sit in the hallway and wait for her, which was a relief since that meant Wyatt and Caroline could stay with me. Both of them had taken their places at my sides, only moving when a doctor or a nurse came in to manage my pain or to facilitate furthering my care. Due to being a minor, many of their big decisions had to wait until my mom arrived, which was probably why Wyatt sighed loudly in relief at my mom's arrival.

"Ma'am, she is down the hall. I can take you to her room," Jessica spoke up; her voice seemed further away than my mom's. "I'm one of her friends from school, Jessica Chang. Caroline told me to wait outside here for you."

It was only seconds before they joined us and before Mom's face was suspended over mine with her hands gently cradling my face. My eyes finally cleared enough to see through them, but the neck brace still limited my movements. "Felicity! You have no idea how badly you scared me. What the heck happened to you?"

I tried to speak up and reassure her, but my mouth had not recovered from its dryness, so again, nothing came out. Thankfully, Caroline had gotten used to speaking for me, so she approached my side and reviewed everything the nurse had told her. "She is doing okay. They said that she is completely stable. The party at my house got a little out of hand. She was running up the stairs after me and slipped, which ended with her falling into the banister and crashing down onto the lower-level floor. They are waiting for you to get here before they take her back for an x-ray, but they think that she has some broken ribs and possibly a broken leg. She was also holding a glass cup, which broke underneath her when she fell. They have already gone through and extracted the pieces of broken glass since they were all on the surface. They also stitched up the openings and will prescribe a cream for the scarring once the stitches are out so that hopefully there is nothing but a faint line when she is all healed."

It was as if the floodgates of Caroline's mouth had been opened as she relayed in perfect detail all of the information she had told the doctors and what the doctors had told her and Wyatt. Her hand came up to hold onto mine as she spoke, and I took notice of its slight tremor.

"They also gave her something for the pain, which is why she keeps falling asleep." Wyatt chimed in from his seat beside the bed. The guilt from my accident was radiating off him, which was probably why he had let Caroline take point on the conversation with my mom. I had overheard the conversation between Caroline and Wyatt, where she accused him of being the reason I had been on the second floor and near the railing in the first place.

Caroline pointed out the call button beside my head. "I can push the button for the nurse so that she can go over the care details with you. She should probably know that you are here so that the doctor can come back in."

Mom gently lifted a finger to her lips to suggest Caroline quit with her nervous chatter. "Honey, you have done a great job. Thank you for helping Felicity get here and for handling the doctors." She reached across me to fidget with the stiff, scratchy hospital-issued blanket someone had thrown over me. It was nothing compared to the uncomfortableness of my short hospital gown. "I'm so sorry it took me so long to get here. I was out with your aunt Lola, and the freeway had the worst traffic. I feel so bad that I wasn't here for you."

My aunt Lola was mom's best friend, her version of Caroline. Often, when I was spending the night with Caroline, Mom went off to spend time with her. They both got to celebrate being young, beautiful, and kid-free, even if it was only for one night at a time. She lived two hours away, so the addition of traffic made her drive closer to three hours.

"We have it all settled. I called my dad, and he said that because the accident happened at our house, he would handle all medical expenses." Carolina picked up right where she left off, going off some imaginary checklist in her head. "I lied to the nurses that we were related so that we could come back with her. The staff here said that you were welcome to stay the night with her, or I can do that so that you can go home and rest. I know that you must be exhausted. I won't be able to sleep tonight, so I am happy to spend the night here so she's not alone."

Mom shook her head rapidly. She softly ran her fingers through my tangled mass of hair; it had been in a braid beneath the wig, so when that had come off, it left me with a mess, and my fall only made it worse. "There is no way I could leave my baby here, but I appreciate the offer." She turned an eye to Wyatt; her distaste for him was clear. "What do you say about finding me some coffee? Two creams, one sugar. Please and thank you."

Wyatt agreed to get her coffee and disappeared quietly. I could hear him ask Jessica if she wanted anything. After delivering my mom, she returned to the waiting room to wait for Kaden and Nolan since they were still expecting to make their arrival.

Caroline and Mom both chose to take a seat, holding my hands while they spoke over me.

A tall man in a white coat strolled into the room with a charismatic smile. "How are we doing this fine evening?" His brunette hair had been gelled to a perfected style, and he looked only twenty minutes into the 12-hour-long shift. "I just spoke to the doctor who did your stitches, and they said that you're going to heal great! We all feel really good about this. At most, you will have a slight scar, which will tell a great story."

Mom patted my hand sympathetically as if trying to shoulder the burden of this news. "Something was said about her being given a scar cream? Will that take away the mark?" She hadn't even seen the stitches yet and was already worried about the scars and how long they were going to stay. They should be something that I cared about, but somehow, I couldn't work up the energy, knowing that healing my leg had to be my top priority.

The doctor smiled reassuringly in my direction but turned his attention back to my mom, recognizing she was the one freaking out. "You will barely be able to see them. Now, let's get her off to an x-ray. We need to assess her leg and ribs." As if they had been waiting at the door, a team of nursing aides and nurses came into the room, unlocking the bed and wheeling me towards the x-ray room.

That was only the first of many tests run before they finally decided that my ribs were bruised, my leg was broken in two places, and thankfully, my head suffered no damage from the fall other than some surface bruising that they claimed would take a few short weeks to heal. My leg was going to need surgery; a metal plate and a few screws would be required to ensure that it healed properly.

Mom failed to fully settle down even after she had been reassured that I would be just fine and that I would need time to rest and to heal. She continued to pace the room unless a doctor or a nurse were there. Then she stood, staring over their shoulder so that she could take in all they were doing. She made sure to ask no less than a hundred questions, and all their answers were written down in her trusted notebook so she could return to it later.

It took a few nurses before one of them noticed what she was doing, or she was the first one who cared to say anything about it. She swiftly tucked a piece of blonde hair behind her ear and came closer to where I lay in the bed and where Mom stood, overlooking it all. "I can write down a list of things you, or anyone, taking care of Felicity needs to be aware of. The biggest issue will be infection from the incisions and any bed sores. She will be bed-bound for a while after the surgery on her leg. When she is back home, it would be best to have her crutches readily accessible at all times. It would also be best that she is on a single floor, not going up and down a flight of stairs."

"Would she be okay on the couch then?" Our two-bedroom, two-bathroom house had two floors, with the bedrooms upstairs, so unless we were going to pull out the old blow-up mattress, the couch would be the best option. "Or will the breaks between the cushions cause issues for her healing?"

The nurse, Ana, looked barely seconds older than eighteen but had the gusto of someone about fifty years older. She took command of the room and my frantic mother. "No, she will be just fine. If there is any discomfort, you can put pillows in those cracks. I can talk to some of the other nurses about getting you a detailed care plan so that when you return home, you can ensure everything is set up. Please feel free to ask me any questions you have."

Mom took that comment in stride, and her questions didn't slow down, not even as the week went on. She barely slowed down as a nurse wheeled me out to the car with a brand-new wheelchair that I was given to make my transition back to walking easier now that I was getting to go home.

* * *

"Honey, you need to make sure to rest." Mom fluffed the pillow behind my head and straightened my blanket, intending to make me magically feel better with the straight lines. "Can I get you something to drink or eat? You need to make sure to eat something. I can make mac and cheese or maybe some top ramen? There might be some vegetables in the fridge that we could do some dip with."

"That sounds good. Do you mind making me some ramen?" I wasn't hungry, but sitting around made her anxious, and her shuffling around me caused me to experience the same emotions.

I had sat on this couch for over a month with Mom and Caroline, who were switching off shifts of caring for me. The crutches that the hospital had given me made navigating my house easier than the wheelchair had been, but not by much, so I was grateful for their assistance.

Mom reminded me to lift my leg and put a pillow beneath the cast, raising it up to help reduce the swelling, just as the nurses directed her. My ribs had healed nicely, and my stitches were out. Now, Mom diligently applies the cream to them twice daily, hoping they would not leave red scars. "Caroline will be coming over as soon as school gets out. You should probably nap before she gets here. I know that she has a million things she wants to go over with you before you return to school next week."

Caroline had made it her mission to keep me updated with all of the Riverside Preparatory gossip while I was away, using the excuse that she needed to drop off my classwork. Not surprisingly, a lot of the gossip had to do with me and my tragic fall from the Calloway balcony. A few hundred people witnessed it that night, and the rest of the school heard about it by the following day. That combination meant hundreds of versions of the story; everyone shared theirs as if it were new news. Thankfully, Caroline was kind enough to spare me the details of all the rumors.

Wyatt hadn't come to see me since the night of the party. Not long after Mom arrived, he left, returning home with Nolan and Kaden, saying something about needing to clean the house before their parents got home. Caroline had been surprisingly tight-lipped on why he hadn't come by, although she had passed over the excuse that their dad had lost it over the broken banister and the house party. While she was here taking care of me, Wyatt had to pay the price by working every day at the company. She claimed that he was in debt to their dad, and he was not being kind about how Wyatt would pay him back.

The ringing of my phone broke through the silence; it was a cheesy country song that sung about falling in love. Caroline's eyebrow was raised in surprise, quickly putting the clues together as to who it was on the other end of the phone. "Is that your ringtone for Wyatt?"

After getting over her initial shock, she surprisingly supported Wyatt and me dating. I wasn't so sure you could call it dating still with his lack of effort. I had reached out to him a few times, but all my messages went unanswered.

"Yeah, I don't know what happened to my phone though. Can you help me find it?" I had been confined to the couch for weeks now, and the pillows had become fused with my body. Mom had brought in TV trays from Aunt Lola's house so that I could have a place for water, my phone, and the remote, but somehow, I still managed to lose one of those things every day. Thankfully, Caroline tracked the phone down with a smile, choosing to laugh at me and my inability to do anything for myself.

Caroline handed the phone to me and then started to leave the room. She must have seen the look on my face because she had begun to defend herself. "Don't be offended that I'm leaving the room. I don't know if I can handle you and my brother sharing sweet words back and forth." Caroline had also confined herself to the couch beside me for most of my recovery and had made herself at home here. As she walked towards the kitchen, I heard her mimic us, "You hang up first, no you hang up first." as if that was really what we sounded like or something we had said.

Before answering the phone, I waited until she was fully out of the room. "Hey Wyatt. I'm happy to hear from you."

"Felicity. How are you feeling?" His voice was muffled as if he was far away from the phone.

My fingers found the frayed edges of the blue blanket in my lap to fidget with while we spoke, my nervous energy finding itself at home. "A lot better. My leg is the only thing still bothering me, and the doctor said that it's healing great. I still can't leave the house yet, but will return to school in two weeks. Maybe you could stop by to see me? I would love to see you."

It was awkward and stiff as I listened to his breathing, as he seemed to ponder what to say next. "I don't know if that is possible. I've been really busy lately between working for my dad and practice."

Trying a different approach, I tried not to let that slow me down.

"That's okay. Maybe when I get back to school, we can eat lunch together. I'm serious when I say that I really just want to see you."

His sigh came out swiftly, and it caused my heart to skip a tiny beat, knowing that whatever he was going to say was not good. "Felicity, I'm not sure that will work either. What happened the other night was wrong. No one should have gotten hurt, especially you."

"Wyatt, I'm okay. It wasn't your fault. It was all an accident."

By the way, his breathing failed to slow down, and I could tell he did not feel that way. "No, it was my fault, which is why we can't do this anymore. I need to grow up and get my life in order. I need to stop messing around, especially now that college is right around the corner. Once I get there, everything will be different, and there is going to be all of these new opportunities that I'm not going to want to miss out on, and I won't be able to do them if we are still together."

"Messing around? What are you talking about?" I couldn't wrap my mind around Wyatt being someone who was messing around with his life when he was constantly striving for more, especially striving to be better than his father.

"College is right around the corner, and I need to get ready for it." His voice was trailing off in the way it did when he got distracted. I could picture him running his hand through his blonde wavy hair until it was a tousled mess.

I tried to collect myself and the fury of emotions that I was feeling. "Isn't that why we study each day? I thought I was helping you get ready for it." His excuse didn't make any sense, but I could tell it probably had much to do with his father. "Why are you pushing me away?"

He laughed in a sinister fashion that caused my heart to sink further into my chest. "Felicity, you're not getting it. I'm not pushing you away; I am using this as an opportunity to change things. I am leaving for college soon, and there is too much out there for me to be held back by some high school girlfriend."

After the slightest pause, the phone hung up, and my broken

heart was accompanied by the dial tone that plagued the silence of my tears.

"Felicity, what is wrong?" Caroline shouted through the room, causing me to drop the phone back into my lap. She stomped over to where I sat and joined me on the couch, the cross expression on her face not leaving now that she had noticed I was in distress. "What did he say to you?"

"He broke up with me."

Her gasp almost caused me to giggle, as did the expression that would not leave her face. "Why would he break up with you?" She waved her hands in frustration. "What a selfish idiot he is. I am ashamed to be related to such a butthead."

Caroline reached behind us and grabbed the box of tissues, giving them over to me since I had a healthy amount of snot and tears exiting my face at an alarming rate. "He said he needed to get his life together, and I was only holding him back. Then, as he hung up, he commented that he didn't want a high school girlfriend holding him back."

She let out a gasp again, her eyes only growing wider as I spoke. "I know you are hurting, but if this were on TV, it would be gold! This is better than when Warner breaks up with Elle in *Legally Blonde*."

She was right too. Things like this never seemed to happen in real life like they often occur in movies.

"I just don't understand what caused this shift. Everything was fine before the party." I knew I was probably wrong, but I could only assume it has something to do with us coming to the party and exposing us as a couple.

Caroline was of another opinion, and whatever it was, I could tell that it made her angry. The tension growing between her eyebrows caused there to be a few dozen wrinkles. "I imagine that this is my dad's doing. He probably pushed him into making this decision because this does not sound like anything Wyatt would say. He just wants every part of his life to be miserable like his own."

I could tell there was more she wanted to say, but she hesitated, as if what she was about to say was too much for me to handle. My words came out frantic. "What? Just say it."

"I know that I told you our dad lost it over the broken banister, but it is so much worse. He started talking to our mom about sending Wyatt away to a new school, a military academy, where Wyatt could get some sense of responsibility. I think he probably threatened him with something like that, and this is the only way that Wyatt felt he could appease our dad."

As much as I wanted to find relief in her words that he felt it was his best option, I just couldn't believe that if someone loved me as much as they claimed they did, they would be so willing to walk away.

When Mom came home, I retold the story, tears brimming in my eyes, although I did feel a little better having the two of them beside me. It was even better when Mom ordered Chinese food for us to eat while we watched Legally Blonde, which Caroline considered the best breakup revenge movie of all time.

Somehow, as we watched Elle Woods win the big case and graduate law school, I felt peace knowing that it was going to be okay, especially if I had the two of them beside me.

Chapter 9

The Wedding

Caroline was a nervous wreck, and the status of her fingernails showed it.

I had heard about their fate long before I saw them, which did nothing to hide the surprise on my face when I took them in. I had gone downstairs to check on the cake I had made, and I had overheard MaryAnn's disappointment that I hadn't stopped Caroline from picking away as if that was something I could control.

I didn't regret my decision to leave her with the other bridesmaids since the cake was a crucial part of the wedding and the only part that I was solely responsible for. I had tasked two of my staff members to deliver it since I had stayed with Caroline at the Calloway house the night before.

I let the two of them open the box while I braced myself for disappointment, already going over all the ways I could fix any frosting issues that were sure to come from the box and transport.

My eyes opened slowly so I could take it in, and the sight of my masterpiece sent a mighty thrill through me. I had worked on it until after midnight the day before, knowing that today, my maid of honor duties had to come first.

Caroline had two requests for her cake: white and tiered. MaryAnn also had two requests: massive and caused all the rest of the guests to be jealous.

The four-tiered cake sat before me; it was the largest I had ever made and the most decorated. White Buttercream, Caroline's favorite, was the base of the cake, with matching white piping and large white frosted roses that were the showstopper I would always be proud of. Quickly, I took out my phone and took half a dozen photos of them, promising myself that I would add them to my website as soon as the wedding was over.

"We need to get this out there and displayed. Make sure it is situated on the stand and centered in front of the window." My direction was met with hopeful smiles. Both of my employees were college students who were grateful for a job requiring only a small amount of participation over the weekend. Because I was in the wedding party, this was the most participation they had been required to do, and I knew they were both grateful for the overtime. "If you get confused, find my mom. Avoid the mother of the bride. I can't afford the therapy you will need if she yells at you."

Both laughed as if I was making a joke, and I let them think that I was as they pushed the cake towards the ballroom, where I could only hope my mother was waiting for them.

I felt a strong sense of relief that she was in charge of everything tonight as I snuck past the kitchen staff where Emsley was commanding her troops. I paused only to steal an apple from her basket. I could immediately tell she caught me, winking in my direction as I snuck up the servant's staircase.

Wyatt had snuck through earlier in the week and had strung a line of motion reactive lights, knowing that I would be using it often today when there would be so many people in the house that I would be trying to avoid.

I was grateful for his actions when he told me about it, but even more so today as I raced up and down the steps and people asked me to join them in different areas of the house. Caroline had appointed me to be her right-hand man by choosing me to be her maid of honor, but that was only magnified today when she had been told to stay in her bedroom so no one saw her and ruined the surprise.

Sneaking into the bride's bedroom was easy with how many people were in there, so I kept close to the wall mostly to avoid Mary-Ann, who stood in the middle of the room with a snarled look on her face, directing orders to the series of maids who had been employed for the day.

No one went through maids as quickly as MaryAnn Calloway; it was as if there was a revolving door in the back of the house, so none of them were faces I was familiar with. They had a few that had lasted longer since they figured out the situation well enough to keep most of their business away from the keeper of the house whenever possible, so those were the ones who were downstairs working with my mom.

I snuck up the side until I was closer to where Caroline stood, and I tried to seamlessly join the chaos by filling up a champagne glass and bringing it to her waiting hand. "Hey Hun, how are you feeling?"

She gave the glass a long drink and took a deep breath. The entire goal for the day was to ensure she had a happy and carefree buzz, not drunk, which is why I had been tasked to be her official drink manager so that it didn't go over that line.

"I'm okay." Caroline did not sound as confident as she wanted to, which she confirmed by the second swig of her glass. "I don't know why I am nervous. I know that he loves me and that this is what he wants. I know that the party is going to be beautiful. These are all things that I know to be true."

I tried to be as reassuring as possible. "I am pretty sure that it is a rule that you must be nervous on your wedding day, no matter how confident you feel about everything."

Her beauty team entered the room in a flurry, putting their hair and makeup boxes down as they rushed to her side. They covered her with their infectious happy energy, which seemed to be everything she needed to feel better. They were the same crew as last time and seemed very comfortable to be back here, throwing their stuff out of their bags onto the makeup table before them.

I watched in amazement as they transformed her before our eyes. I worked on myself in the bathroom mirror, fixing the rest of my makeup and spraying enough hairspray to ensure the curls would not move from their position.

MaryAnn decided to get ready in her bedroom with her beauty team, giving Caroline some alone time with her bridesmaids and some space away from her mother. I knew MaryAnn had much to do with why Caroline was picking away her fingernails.

All of the other bridesmaids fixed their hair and makeup on the other side of the room, using all of the mirrors available to ensure that we would be able to get downstairs and that the wedding would start on time.

* * *

Caroline shook her body again, trying to lose the nervous energy that she had been keeping there. If she hadn't been in a tight corset, she probably would have started meditating or doing yoga, maybe even going for a quick jog to lessen the tension she was feeling. "Tell me that I've got this. I just need to hear that once from you. If anyone else said it to me, I wouldn't believe them."

"You got this." I hugged her tight, whispering in her ear so that no one else overheard. We were standing at her bedroom door, waiting for our walk down the stairs. "And if you don't want to have this, we can always make a break for it. That is always going to be an option."

The wedding guests were all seated in the ballroom, and the rest of us congregated at the bottom of the stairs so that we could all go inside the way we had practiced the night before.

Caroline and I wrapped our arms around each other, making it difficult to walk down the stairs, but we didn't let go of each other. Growing up, we had done it a million times, not wanting to part until we were at the door where I had to leave. Somehow, this felt like a heightened level of a final goodbye.

It felt symbolic to walk down the stairs this way now. I was now walking her to where she had to leave me behind in the bachelorette life as she headed into the world of marriage.

She had tasked me to get her to her dad at the bottom of the stairs, which felt like the greatest gift she could have ever given me.

As soon as our feet hit the bottom step, I kissed her cheek sincerely and squeezed her hand in mine. "You are the most beautiful bride! Thank you for being my best friend."

She squeezed me back just as tightly. "I love you!"

I let go of her and found my place beside Wyatt, who took my hand in his to link our arms. He leaned down to kiss my cheek, giving it all the same level of emotion as the one I gave Caroline. "Are you ready for this?"

His tone let me know he was talking about more than the dreaded walk down the aisle. The toast I expected to give was looming over my head like a bad dream.

The beginning of the wedding party walked towards the door, and the music started. I watched their timed steps and tried to keep track of the count so we would stay at the same speed when it was Wyatt's and my turn.

Slowly, one by one, all the other bridesmaids and groomsmen made their way to the altar, and it was time for Wyatt and I to make our way down the same path. All of the pairs had laced their arms together, which was a relief as it allowed me to lean onto him and for him to hold me steady as he led the way.

As we reached the end, standing the closest to the altar, Wyatt pressed his lips to mine in a way that held more than a million promises for our future and what his change of heart meant.

The flower girl came up the aisle alongside the ring bear, and then the music changed, signaling the bride's arrival. The entire crowd stood to face her, and there was a loud gasp that went through the room as they took in her beautiful wedding gown, its v shape in the front was accompanied by the long slit going up her leg. The white roses in her hand contrasted the gorgeous tan that made up her exposed skin.

There was a slight rumble of a whisper as people commented on her look, and I could hear Richard let out a "Wow" of his own, which made my eyes water, just getting a small glimpse into how much he loves her.

Their ceremony was beautiful, their vows echoing their love for each other, and as they leaned in to seal their kiss, the crowd erupted in celebration. The rest of us watched them walk out of the ballroom and back into the hallway, where they would take some photos of the two of them with the photographer MaryAnn had hired.

Wyatt fidgeted with his hair and came back for me once the family photos were done, grabbing my hand and helping me shuffle through the crowd to where the tables and chairs were ready for people to enjoy small appetizers. While we ate, the hired staff was tasked with changing out the bench seating of the wedding into the grand ballroom for dancing and dinner.

Many of the guests walked in circles around the room, making good use of the hour to chat with those around us. After all of the wedding celebrations this year, the guests had become close, all getting to know each other and becoming comfortable with striking up a conversation.

Wyatt took me around the room on his arm, choosing to help me build my business while we had the opportunity. He proudly proclaimed to everyone we spoke to that I was the one who baked the cake, and they all needed to try it before the night was over.

We sat beside each other as we ate dinner, his arm pressed against my back, causing a rush of goosebumps to overcome my body whenever we moved.

There was a slight lull in the room as all the guests ate their dinner, meaning it was my queue to stand up to speak. Taking the microphone in hand, I smiled at the tables surrounding us, my normal queasiness overcoming me and a small bead of sweat coming across my brow that I tried to ignore. "Hi everyone! I bet you are so excited to hear from me again." A chuckle came from the guests, which reassured me that the joke was the right thing to say. "I want to thank you all for coming out today to share this joyful occasion. I had the joy of watching Richard and Caroline fall in love over the last few years, and just like all of you, I have been here to celebrate all of the wedding festivities, seeing how much love they have for each other."

I carried on for a few moments, sharing memories and happy moments from growing up with Caroline and how excited I was for them to move forward with their lives. I let the last of my words settle before returning to my seat, quickly gulping back the water I desperately needed.

Wyatt immediately took my place, sharing his memories of the bride and groom. He and Richard had been college roommates, which was how Richard had come to know Caroline, so his stories helped complete the circle of their love story since I only knew them once they had started dating. Richard had returned to our hometown to be closer to Caroline.

"I ask you all to raise your glass to celebrate the bride and groom!" Wyatt lifted his champagne glass in the air before taking a sip. Everyone before us did the same motion before shouting out their cheers and clapping while Richard and Caroline pressed their lips together tightly in a blissful newlywed kiss.

The band started up a happy tune, and my wedding date reached out his hand for mine. "Flick, may I have this dance?"

Wyatt led me to the dance floor where he leaned in close to me and lovingly placed his lips against my forehead, "I have a feeling that throughout our lives, I will get the opportunity to re-fall in love with you as many times as there are stars in the sky." He moved our bodies back and forth with the soft melody of the music, showing off his skill and allowing me to follow along. "I'm just sorry it took me so long to get here and to get back to you."

I couldn't help but fall into his lips, feeling their warmth press against mine. He deepened it softly, nibbling onto my bottom lip to get a reaction out of me. "Wyatt Calloway. You are more than I was ever expecting."

"Since the invention of the kiss, there have been five kisses that were rated the most passionate, the most pure." He paused to draw out the dramatics, knowing it would kill me a little to wait even a second longer than I thought was necessary. I had the line memorized from all my time watching the movie; somehow, the words coming out of his mouth felt like so much more than the narrator on the show. "This one left them all behind."

And then he kissed me. It was the most passionate kiss we had ever exchanged. His hands rushed to the sides of my face, going as far as to reach into my hairline. Wyatt bit my lip, pulling it into his mouth to suck on it for a second before releasing it, but he wasn't done there. He pulled me in tighter to his body until our chests were pressed together, and the beating of his heart became the only thing I could hear. His left hand went from my hair down the contours of my body until it rested on my hip, finding the place he loved the most.

His fingers flexed against my body, and I melted further into him, finally feeling at home.

"This is true love. You think this happens every day?"
-Westly, The Princess Bride

Ari. I don't remember how we became friends, but I imagine it was similar to Felicity and Caroline, with one of us announcing the friendship and the other just happy to be there. We decided to be partners in crime and never looked back. I don't think either of us realized that we were choosing our sisters for life at nine years old, but I am so glad we were brave enough to do that because life wouldn't be the same without you!

Cowboy, your support means the absolute world to me! You are always in my corner and have my back. There is no one else I would want to take on this world with and no one else that I would want to raise our babies with. I am so grateful for all that you do for me and for our little family. You are my hero today and every day!

Momma, thank you for taking the time to edit my book and for taking time out of your busy life to support my dream! I am so proud of all the things you have done this year and for going after the things you want! You are such an inspiration to me and my siblings; we are so lucky to have you as our momma!

To my amazing parents, thank you for being the first to buy my book and for always supporting me!!! I would have never found my voice as an author if you had not constantly supported all of my dreams and for fueling my book addiction. I am so grateful for you! Please know how much I love you!

To everyone who took a shot on my book and Beta read for me, thank you for taking that time to support me! I appreciate you so much!

THANK YOU to all the people who told me it was okay to quit nursing school and chase my real passion! My happiness is because of your support and encouragement.

Keeper of the Magic

Trena VanHoff

Preface

There was an overwhelming opinion in our towns that I was different, or at least, that the women in my family were different.

It was that sixth sense that told one to be cautious. That is what caused the hair on their necks to rise when they saw us nearby; it was a warning to be aware that has been ingrained in the human body since the beginning of time.

It was the way that trivial things always went our way that caused people to start looking twice in our direction. It was the way that neither of my sisters ever had to fix their hair in the mornings. My mom never worried about any meal that had to be prepared or the house getting cleaned. I suppose that it might be the way that my grandma always had the right answer instantly with the tools to go along with it. I had come to realize that the trivial things that had always seemed to go our way were not a happy accident or a stroke of good luck, but instead, it was that each moment was choreographed in our own way to keep everyone else in the dark of all that we were truly capable of.

While the world thought my family had just a little bit more luck than the family next door, it was actually that they were witches with a bloodline from Salem.

Descendants of the witches they couldn't burn.

And I had that magic in myself as well.

Chapter 10

Keeper of the Magic- Chapter One

"There is one important thing to remember, Blair Marie, and that is that this is your destiny, but it does not come to any of us naturally. This will not come to you without putting in a lot of hard work."

My sisters and I always knew Grandma was being serious when she decided to use our middle names during one of her lectures. By taking that small second, she let us know the berating was made only for us, as was the disappointment that rang through her words. Thankfully, this was something that all three of us were used to. She often took over the role of disciplinarian during our growing up years and we knew when that line was drawn and when she would draw it.

I tried to be as calm as possible, but her words really were starting to dig in the more she droned on, especially because this had become a regular conversation as my training progressed. She had grown tired of the time this was taking me, just as I had grown tired of spending that time with her; our relationship was beginning to strain the more it fell into the teacher/student role, compared to the normal grandmother/granddaughter role that we were used to.

"I am willing to put in the hard work. I have been putting in the work," I tried to overly emphasize my words to show how sincere I was. "I know that this will not come naturally, I have been putting in the effort and I will continue to try for this."

"You need more than effort. It is sacrifice that brings greatness, and you must constantly be pushing forward with that in mind, or you are never going to get anywhere," she responded. She had lifted her tanned, wrinkled finger and waved it in my face with the intent of driving the point home,

She continued, "I need you to put your entire focus into this and you haven't done that yet." The disappointment she had for us was worse than if she had been mad. I would rather hear her scream than tell me that she was disappointed.

"I understand that," I retorted, "I promise that I do study and work on these, it's just a little harder for me to catch up to the rest of you when I am this far behind."

I wanted her to see my side of it and how hard I really was pushing for this; maybe even have her feel bad for me so that she would give me a break. This was not the first time we had this conversation, and it wouldn't be the last if I continued to be behind the rest of our Coven. My sisters also started at the bottom, but they weren't the last witch of their line. Our Coven can't cast as powerful of spells until I have mastered my magic.

"I don't think you know how much I have put into this," I finished.

She didn't change the expression on her face, it was as tight as ever and full of frustration that she wasn't even trying to hide from me like she had done in the beginning: "I do not want to hear excuses. What I want is results."

"I truly have been studying every night, putting in that time whenever I can around my shifts at the shop," I tried to explain to her why it was taking so long. Explain that I was struggling with keeping my attention on our lesson, the magic still felt too foreign to me, and she was clearly getting frustrated with the lack of results.

"There is still so much that I need to learn and that is a little overwhelming."

She kept going as if I hadn't said anything either time, which wasn't uncommon when it came to her lectures. She had a one-track mind, and she was not going to stop talking until you at least felt the minimum level of her disappointment.

"You must put in the effort if you want the reward, and I can see that you want it. What I can't see is how hard you are willing to work for it and that is the part that I need to see the most!"

If I couldn't manage to get it together for at least this spell before the day was over, then I didn't know what I was going to do or, even worse, what they were going to do to me. Being exiled from our Coven seemed like a possibility if she continued to look at me like that.

My mother was at her wits end when it came to training me after days of endless lessons that didn't seem to go anywhere. It didn't help that magic was the only thing that we discussed when we were together, and my lack of progression was frustrating her with each passing day. Living together meant that the lectures never ended, even if she tried to. It was hard for her to switch off between her role as mother and the one she was forced to have as my teacher. I could tell that Grandma was close to her breaking point as well, as I had been handed over to her and had become her responsibility to deal with the last few weeks.

Grandma did not wait for my response, instead just continued with her lecture. It was as if she had a goal to say a minimum word count every minute and tried to use as many as possible while she was with me.

"So let us break this down further. The word *otium* and *pax* might, in theory, have a similar meaning. Because it is in Latin you have to ensure that you are using the right one. You have to understand that Latin uses many different words to communicate the same message, but that is the way to turn a precious house cat into a ferocious lion. At one point they can both be considered tame and at peace; there is a chance that one of them will change their attitude and now you are chasing a large lion through the town and calling it fluffy. That is not a battle that you would win, I can confidently tell you that one," Grandma explained firmly.

She held up the spell book so that I could read it while I cast the spell. She had a hope that I would have the words memorized before the next time that we came together to practice (it was yet to happen) but the hope was still there, nonetheless.

At least I could say that she had faith in me.

"I understand that." I repeated the words once more, trying to put as much sincerity in my voice as possible. Although, her tone made me feel very discouraged about the entire conversation and my ability to do this.

This was not the first time she had tried to get me to understand the importance of using all the words correctly in a spell even if I were yet to see anything wrong happen. She claimed that was only because I do not hold the power yet to do any real damage and that I had to learn this lesson before I was that strong. It was like learning how to walk before you learned how to run, frustrating, but more useful than I wanted to admit, especially to her.

Grandmother was right about one other thing and that was my need to study the books more and to get the language to the point of, at least, what could be considered a general understanding, which was the part I continued to struggle with. Latin was a *complicated* language, and it was easy to get confused when you add in the element of magic— it intensifies the need to get it right, which only made me more nervous. I had spent *endless* hours studying the language already and it was barely coming together to make any sense at all.

"While it does not matter as much right now because you are still copying the spells of our ancestry and your Coven members, it is going to matter when you are creating your own spells. Now why don't we go again from the top once more." Grandma might have been frustrated with me, but she did believe in me, and I was going to have to ride on that blind faith until I had that same faith in myself.

"You got it this time; I can feel it."

I could feel a shake in my hands and my heart was beating a little faster than it should. Fingering my amethyst amulet, to calm myself down I took a long, deep breath and began to try the spell once more, with a small prayer that it would finally go right.

My poor dog sat in the middle of the table staring back at me, thankfully blissfully unaware of what she was being put through. Grandmother had put her there in replacement of the normal witch's Cat like the one that the spell was created for. I do not know if my dog, Jinx, would turn into a ferocious lion or closer to a dangerous wolf if I mixed up the words, but I also did not want to be the one to find out.

The spell I was trying to master today was one that accompanied training an animal, getting them to calm down so they could focus. Grandma was the one who suggested using the spell on my puppy who was not taking to the potty-training idea despite the last few months that I had tried to enforce it. I personally did not feel like this was a chance I was willing to take on my baby and by the look in Jinx's eyes I could tell that she felt the same way about the situation, her anxiety levels rising to the state that mine were.

"My pet is sweet and deserves a treat, make my pet pax for she runs at her max."

I repeated the words slowly and carefully, trying to remember the rhyme I had studied so diligently last night before bed, refraining from looking down at the book my grandma was holding in her hands — mostly to prove to myself that I could do it. I tried to focus on Jinx while I moved my wand around her head.

The tip of my wand had a faint golden glow that came off it as I cast a spell on the small white puppy. Thankfully, the only physical reaction that she gave was the slight tilt of her tiny head, probably in wonder of what I was doing to her.

"Does every spell have to rhyme like that? I know that I haven't written any of my own yet, but all the rhymes seem like they would get old fast and that you would run out of words to use," I had initially been encouraged to ask questions, but sometimes the look on Grandma's face said otherwise, this being one of those times.

"Your sister, Penelope, created this spell when it came to a sweet calico that ran around your grandparent's farm so that she could catch it. Her goal was to convince your parents that she could have it as a pet," Grandmother smiled softly before quickly removing the expression on her face, moving forward as fast as possible from her comment about my father as if it was something that burned her tongue. This was never talked about, so the fact that she casually brought him up surprised me even if it was *just* in passing.

"Not every spell has to rhyme, but it does help you remember it when it does," She explained, "When you make your own spells, you don't have to use them unless you want to. Most do it as a way to remember the spell, just like a nursery rhyme; the cadence helps it stick."

"It doesn't help me remember it!" The rules of witchcraft were exhausting to say the least and it seemed like every time I turned around there was a new one that I had to follow, "It almost makes it harder for me to remember what word is supposed to come next."

"Honey, your concentration must stay with the spell or else it will not ever work." She even went as far as to reach up, grab my chin, and move my head down to where my eyes would be put on Jinx who sat in front of me, "You must be able to put your entire attention on your spell, having it memorized because one day you will have to say these in your head instead of having a book there to read off of."

"Okay, I understand that."

When the women of my family sat me down on my eighteenth birthday to share our family legacy with me, each of them moved forward to give me a part of the magic I had patiently waited years for. It was also then that I was able to become one with the curse that had a hold over each member of my Coven.

The curse started during the Salem Witch Trials. It was then that the women of the Bradbury family, the witches, came together and decided that the only way to protect their family was to freeze the magic that the women held. They hoped that by doing that it would protect it from being taken by someone's death as the villagers were willing to go after anyone in search of the witches they feared. Their desperation caused them to turn on those they had previously considered friends. The witches in my Coven protected themselves by only allowing one woman in the family to hold the magic until she felt that the next members of the family were ready for the gift. This is why, to this day, we were only given the magic once we were old enough to handle the responsibilities that had to come with it. It was a lot easier to hide the magic when only one person was having to be careful with it and even easier than that when it was hidden in the oldest women who could easily keep it away from the eyes of others even when they were looking closely.

This witch, the one who held all the magic, became the matriarch of our family and was known from then on as the Keeper of the Magic. As she was the oldest and the wisest, the Keeper of the Magic was tasked with raising up the next line of witches and the secret was to only be kept within their family. It was an especially critical position that came with great power.

The first Keeper of the Magic, Andromeda, was able to keep her family safe by keeping the magic within her control until she felt ready to share it. Andromeda slowly started giving back to her daughters as the villagers stopped coming after them. Her mistake being that she gave it to her youngest daughter, Annabelle, too early. She had a plan to add her to their Coven of witches so that they would be more powerful as the threat of the Salem Witch Trials was towering over their heads with many of the young women in town being sentenced to death.

Annabelle was born a simple girl with big dreams of much more than what her modest life held for her. Her father was long gone before she knew him, a sickness later known as smallpox causing his death. This was long before the witches understood recovery magic:

when they would be able to save those from worldly illnesses and afflictions; in their world, there was nothing that could be done. His untimely death left her mother, Andromeda, alone with her three young daughters to raise on a small farm where they kept their modest horses and a few lanes of vegetables that helped them make it through the long winter seasons. They all relied on their human skills far more than their magic, since everyone was watching for magic during this time.

All Annabelle wanted was to impress and marry the mayor's son, Henry. She had a theory that if she were to marry the mayor's son, then the magic would not have to be hidden anymore. They could be free to wield their magic whenever and however they wanted. She would be powerful in her social stature as well as in her magic so they would not have to hide from the people who feared the witches, those who hunted them, because she would rule over them all. She saw the power she was given by her mother as an opportunity to do this.

The young girl used the magic she had been given to her advantage, running the town rampant as fast as she could. She was set out to ensure that none of the other girls in the town would get the chance to get to Henry while she worked on getting him to pick her. Annabelle caused mischief and mayhem everywhere she went, terrorizing everyone that stood in the way of her goals. She started roaring fires, caused great winds, massive floods. All these casualties forced the other families to flee the town for the sake of their crops and harvests, farmers needing to protect their livelihood from the town they lived in. The young witch even went as far as to have the other young women become uncontrollable within their actions, or had things mysteriously happen to their physical appearance such as having their noses grow, lose their hair or it turn grey, or even gain large amounts of weight.

Henry was a very vain man and by doing these things to the other women in their small town, the ones she couldn't manage to send their entire families away, she ensured that no other unwed woman would ever match her beauty or catch his eye in the way that she could.

Andromeda saw the problem within this and what it was going to be for their community. The mother tried to pull her daughter back in, tried to get her to see that damage that she was causing and the danger that it would bring to their family and their Coven. She even went as far as to encourage their Coven of witches to take her magic away from Annabelle, but they all chose against it.

Annabelle's fault was becoming too powerful and too strong, letting her vanity propel her forward. Her actions causing all these things to happen to the other women made the townsfolk become worried for their safety, especially the safety of their daughters, who were obviously the target. It became too much, that even Henry made the decision to run away to sea. He told the town that he would return days before he was to name his bride, as he was convinced that his indecisiveness was what had caused all these things to happen, taking the blame unto himself.

Andromeda was concerned about what the town was going to do to the youngest of her family, as she was the only young woman unaffected by the "bad luck" Henry thought he had brought to their town. As a mother, she worried that they would also find out that her daughter was the reason they were now in search of the mayor's son and why their town was falling to pieces. If they were to discover that she was the cause, it would only be a short amount of time before they were bringing a worn-down rope noose around her neck or building a stake to burn her at as they had done to all the witches they had found before.

As the Keeper of the Magic and the most powerful of them all, Andromeda did the only thing that she thought would protect her family. She cursed her daughter and the remaining unmarried women in our family.

She placed a powerful hex over them that the men in their lives would leave once they had served their purpose, so that they would never get in the way of the magic ever again. A man could never cause another Witch to put their magic in danger for his affection or admiration. She rained this curse down through the generations, casting each woman to be affected by it until a man was worthy of being joined into the Coven, of being trusted with the magic. Only then would the curse be lifted.

This was what caused our uncles, fathers, and grandfather to all disappear long before I came to know of them, only staying long enough to propel the magic to the next generation.

My father was one of the great loves that had left due to the consequences of the curse. He had been a small-town farmer before he met my mother and moved with her to the city. He farmed pigs, cows, even sheep. Every time I asked my mother to tell the story, the details changed. I think this was in a small part so that my sisters and I never had the opportunity to go looking for any other information about him since all our minds were curious and she only was willing to share so much. She worried about who we would find if we went looking. He had a family out there somewhere that she was afraid we would contact and that would only make it messy. It is hard to have a relationship with someone who cannot know the biggest part of you.

The way my father was sent away was like how most of them left, telling my mother that it had all become to much for him. Just as the curse predicted, he was gone before the month was over and my mom was left broken hearted with a family of three young girls to then raise on her own. My mother had thought *somehow* that she had been the one to break the curse, that she had found the one man who was worthy of the curse breaking.

Although I think all the women since the curse had been cast had that very same idea as they met their great loves, she did have a good reason for believing it when the others had not. My father did not disappear the moment my sister Celeste was born and not even four years later when Penelope was born. It was unusual for there to be any more than two daughters born into the Bradbury family and even more unusual for the man to stay after he had produced two daugh-ters. My parents had done this without my father having to leave so my mother thought that the curse was broken, that somehow my father got to stay with them forever.

The day she found that she was to give birth to another Bradbury witch, she sobbed to our ancestors begging for my father to be allowed to stay with them. She cried to the Coven, cried to Andromeda to take the curse from her love and from our family, but I completed the reason my father was sent to her, and he was gone just as quicky as he had come. My mother never fully recovered after that day, just as I imagine none of the Bradbury women before her had.

Agatha, my grandmother, was the current Keeper of the Magic and she was the leader over our Coven, controlling the magic just as the first witch, Andromeda, did centuries before.

She had trained my mother, Endora, and her younger sister, Mira, how to be a witch and the three of them together instructed my sisters, Celeste and Penelope, when they came into their full magic. The five of them were the ones tasked with teaching me of our magic and to bring our family to its full strength of the Coven.

"Now try again," My grandmother coaxed, "Try saying the spell slowly this time around. Remembering to stay as calm as possible, take a deep breath, and now go once more."

It has been taught that we are to use a wand while in training as it has magic from our ancestors and is a way to help produce the spell at a stronger level than what our own magic could do. Then once a witch-in-training was at full power, it was a clever idea to still use one for the harder spells so that it once again could help conduct that power to its strongest form. So, the wand had been attached to my hand throughout all my training with the hopes that one day soon I would be able to leave it behind with the rest of my spell books.

Jinx gave me a scared look, but I felt confident enough to keep on going. I raised the wand and spoke with a strong, steady voice, "My pet is sweet and deserves a treat, make my pet pax for she runs at her max."

There was a shiver that went down my spine as I watched my

sweet puppy jump down from the table and walk herself through the back door, out onto the patch of grass outside.

Grandmother dropped the spell book onto the table and reached out for my hands, clasping them in hers; I could see the look of pride on her face now that I had carried out the spell, "See, I knew that you could do it!"

"Thank you, Grandma for all your help today. I couldn't have done it without you."

"You are right about that, although it was you who did it. I just helped you to focus on the spell."

I didn't know if she meant to be comforting or if she was implying that she had spelled me, but either way I felt successful now that I had done a spell.

"I tell you," She continued, "Your sister Celeste took only a few minutes to accomplish this task, but that could be due to her using an actual cat and, of course, not having their cellphones going off in their back pocket the whole time that they were supposed to be studying their spells."

She was shockingly right, and despite her slight dig at my expense, I knew that I could do this. I would just have to learn how to master the patience needed for the job and remember to silence my cellphone before doing anymore spell casting when Grandma was around.

Grandma gave me her tight twisted smile and I realized that she was not yet done with her proclamation despite the soft pause she gave: "I know that the modern world is compelling, but you need to be willing to put your everything into this. This is it; this is your family destiny, and you need to be willing to step up to it all."

What I did next did not show her that I was truly listening even if I was, because I jumped up out of my seat and proceeded to gather all the spell books up into my hands. I did a quick spell on them to mask their look so that they appeared like math and chemistry textbooks instead of their weathered old covers with Latin scripts.

"That's great, Grandma, it really is! I appreciate you are helping me study and for training Jinx."

"You're leaving so soon?"

"I just must go meet Aunt Mira at the store," I tried to explain, but the look on her face told me that it was falling to deaf ears. She was disappointed in me for leaving so soon after we were done.

"I need you to practice your studies more. You are only going to get out what you are willing to put into this. That means reading over your spells, writing down some of your own, doing some potions or charms in your free time," she tried to emphasize her point by wagging her weathered finger in my face, "You are still treating your magic like it's something you are worried will disappear. It is yours; the magic is in your blood. It is supposed to be another part of you, it should be fluid within your actions."

"I can do that!" I could just barely see the fleeting look of disappointment cross her face as I raced for the backyard, collecting Jinx with me as I hurried out the garden gate, already going to be painfully late for my shift at work even if I ran.

Aunt Mira owned a shop along Palmer Cove where we all lived. It was a small store with an even smaller room in the back where she could take the time to master her craft. In the front of the store, she sold everything from the lavender that helps people to sleep, to the cilantro that we eat.

Her store is called the Corner Shop because it actually is on the corner of the boardwalk, within its obvious cliché it was beautiful at the same time. It is the perfect location for a lot of foot traffic, both for locals and for all the tourists that love the idea of walking along the water. The window displays do wonders to pull people in when there is free time within their day.

Every woman in our family had a very similar look that tied us all together. We all had long black hair, tall slender bodies with olive skin to match. There was a wicked competition between good genetics and the magic that flowed through our veins, but it was probably the magic that helped my aunt and mother to still look like they were in their early thirties.

In a town this small there was not much worry for troublemakers and as a witch, we had a very dependable security system that outdid anything that you would be able to buy at the store. The small bell above the door was alarm enough for Aunt Mira that someone was coming inside.

I found Aunt Mira standing in the middle of the room stirring a large wooden bowl. She was using her magic to mix the ingredients together. The strong fragrance of lavender and rosemary hit me as soon as I turned the corner, and my eyes caught the large bottle of salt sitting on the table beside her, along with half a dozen wooden boxes, glass vials, and jars that held more ingredients for the potion she was mixing.

Grandmother had told me when I received my magic that none of them had found a love potion yet that would combat the curse — even though they had all tried at least once in their youth. Apparently, it was often the first potion that the Bradbury witches made their mission to master on their own. Love is what all young girls hope for, especially when told that they will never get to have it, much less get to keep it. Many gave up after a few tries, but my Aunt Mira was different and more resilient in her pursuit for happiness. She still tried about once a month just in case she cracked the code on a new one, one that would work to bring her love to her and maybe more than that, help her keep him.

Herbs are special, their capabilities depending on how they are used and paired with other ingredients. Aunt Mira was an expert at mixing different herbs together and had an amazing way to find a cure for anything that someone might be looking for: colds, flu, stomach aches and even broken hearts; just not a cure for the curse that hung over all our heads. Rosemary is said to make new things grow, lavender comes with good luck and salt is to be thrown over one's left shoulder to keep out bad luck especially when trying to master a spell of this power; a potion this strong could only come from strong magic. I could only guess the hundreds of other ingredients that she would have added to her potion in hopes of getting it to bring her all that she wanted. There were enough open wooden boxes, mason jars and glass vials beside her that I could throw out a name of any herb and it would be one of them.

While there were negative comments about some of the more interesting beverages she created, there were also rave reviews of the teas that we served. What she was really doing was practicing her love potions on the other sad, single women in our town who were also hoping to find the one. The goal was to find a spell or a potion that worked and when it did, she would take it upon herself — praying that it was strong enough on a witch to break the curse. While she had found a few potions that worked on the women in our town, finding them their true love, none of the potions were ever strong enough to break the Bradbury curse.

She had the opportunity to watch my mom fall in love while young and mournfully watched her raise her babies with the man she loved. It was tremendously hard to watch everything she had ever wanted to be taunted in front of her when she knew how far away from her reach it truly was or even that once she got it, she would not have the chance to keep it. My sisters had both looked for a way to break it, as they were old enough to know my father and to watch the way our mother went through his loss, feeling within themselves what it was like to lose someone in that way. But I do not think that they would break it for themselves even if they were given the chance.

Celeste had gone through the curse herself, been gifted her daughters, and had moved on like it was something of the past. Choosing to focus on the blessing of her daughters and the gift that they were instead of looking backward, saying once that it only held sorrow for everyone. The world is full of single mothers and Celeste saw her role no differently, figuring that magic gave her an edge over the rest and she was confident she was going to be fine.

My other sister, Penelope, had yet to find a love that was strong enough to give her heart to and I often wondered which of my sisters I would take after. If I would be like Celeste and take what was handed to me then quickly move on or if I would act as Penelope does and try to pave my own path with the intention of never getting hurt by never putting my heart out there.

I had always been told that my mother had a softer personality when she was younger, that she was different from the overprotective woman I now knew. That she was wild, fun, and had a way of independent freedom running through her. Losing our dad had changed that in her, took her hope away.

Aunt Mira was unique in a way that no one would ever match. She had hope brewing inside of her so strong that it was overwhelming, it could even make me sick when I had too much exposure. She believed without any doubt in her mind that she was going to find her person one day, that she was going to fall in love and that he would be the one worthy of staying. That does not mean that she was going to be patient about it either, which was something I could relate to.

Aunt Mira would be best categorized as a hippie if I had to choose. While we all had the same pitch-black hair, she wore hers in a long curly mess that had an overwhelming amount of volume, which she often paired with satin headbands woven through the tangles to bring bright colors to the look. She was never seen without a long dress or pants that had enough fabric to put parachutes to shame. Her arms were always adorned with metal bangles that made noise whenever she moved. Aunt Mira was made of something bigger than the stars and she carried herself with that confidence.

"You're here! Do you want to try the new drink that I made up today?" She prompted as she held up a cup as if it were peppermint tea, not that of a potion. "It smells really good, and the extra sugar I mixed in should make it really sweet."

I laughed and quickly shook my head, not even slightly tempted to partake in the drink she was offering, "Not a chance."

Jinx jumped out of my arms and headed for the break room in the back where I had a dog bed waiting for her with an abundance of food and toys to keep her occupied while I was at work. It was a good place for her to run around when I was here with Aunt Mira working so that she wasn't stuck at home.

Lately Aunt Mira had been changing the narrative and coined her herb shop that of a tea store as an easier way to promote the products, get more people in the door, and give herself an alibi for all the teas she was handing out to those hopeless women who came around looking for answers. Aunt Mira figured that with any potion that doesn't work for her, at least it works for the woman in our town, giving her an opportunity to bring that light unto their lives. She had started to make a good name for herself now that she had become more willing to hand out some of the potions within the teas, especially when she gave them a little bit of luck within the leaves. She only worked small magic for it to only seem as if it was good, home-grown ingredients that were helping someone feel better instead of the magic that she infused.

"Grab a kettle from the shelf and start boiling some water for me, please." She continued, "I'm a little behind, I didn't realize how long I had been working."

She was moving even faster than when I first walked into the room. My apron was hanging up on the hook we had on the wall beside the door where I had left it from my shift the day before. I threw it over my head and tied it tight around my waist.

"We need to get started on the Blueberry Sunrise so that there's a lot when the high school lets out. We ran out at noon yesterday and you were not here to help me make more like the slacker that you are," she teased.

Aunt Mira let me use her store as an excuse to earn some extra money, but also a back room where I could study my spells without being interrupted. In a family as large as mine, this meant that there was never a moment alone. It is nice to have Aunt Mira as the other designated black sheep of the family out there watching my back and willing to study with me, especially since she didn't get annoyed when I pestered her with hundreds of questions.

"You could have yelled for me," I retorted, "I would have run out from the back if you were really slammed and helped you." I would hate for her to be taking all the blame as for why I am busy all the time, but then not having the help that she needs to go with it, especially now that the business is growing with each new tea that she puts on the menu.

She just brushed me off with a smile, showing that she was taking the opportunity to tease me, and got back to work on her potion. I watched as she would slowly add the ingredients. She had all of them laying out beside her within reach for when she felt another pinch needed to be added. There was a method to potion making, and while I was not ready for it yet, that did not mean that I did not take the opportunity to watch. Aunt Mira took her time, mixing it slowly to help the flavors blend into a calming combination. She had told me once that if you rush the flavors, the magic of each element would not blend the way they are supposed to.

I got to work putting the tea together. The large pot was on the counter, so I sat it on the stove, turned the burner on, and added water in the hopes that I could quickly get it to boil. I picked up my herbs and spell-books, even taking a moment to study the ones that were laid on the table in person since they were all sitting back there with me. I had to fully go over this specific herbal book and master it before I would be able to make powerful potions like the ones Aunt Mira makes here at the shop. I had learned a lot from studying where there was such exposure to magic. I learned here that a poppy flower is very pretty, but if I added it to a potion, then it could be used to put someone into a gentle sleep. Such as the potion, or what we referred to as tea to the humans, called "Sweet Sleep" that Aunt Mira sold each day.

I heard Aunt Mira exclaim with delight from the front of the store, "This should be a good one! I have got it this time."

"Goodness, Jinx," I whispered to my sweet white puppy who had been curled up at my feet, having fallen fast asleep the second she laid down. She had jumped up at the commotion of Aunt Mira's shouting and was now on guard for whatever was going to happen next, acting like a fierce guard dog despite weighing less than ten pounds. "Do you think she's got it this time? She sounds confident."

Jinx just stared back at me without much to go on in terms of understanding the situation other than a lick of her tongue against my hand. She then silently went back to laying down, easily falling sleep as she had before.

While most witches have a cat, especially a black one when they want to follow the traditions, Jinx had been an unintentional gift from my sister Celeste. My little puppy had been incredibly slim, skin and bones, and was in desperate need of a home, so Celeste had brought her to me thinking I could take the puppy to school with me. She hoped that I could find someone who wanted her, but as soon as she was with me there was no way that I could have given her up to anyone else. It was truly a blessing to have her come into my life, even if my mom did not always appreciate her in the way that I did. She had even threatened to turn her into a statue once or twice upon finding treasures she had brought in from digging holes in the back-yard. Jinx had managed to stay on her good side for four years now and I stopped worrying it was going to happen.

I went back to the front room in time to see a whirlwind of wooden boxes and glass vials floating around me as Aunt Mira used magic to send them all back to their places on the shelves. I stood there with the tea bags in hand to see her twirling around like a little girl, holding the newest potion in a pot above her head like a winner with a trophy.

"You really think that you did it this time?" I asked her, inter-rupting her little dance party. Her smile was overwhelming. "Care-ful, you might spill it all over yourself if you keep jumping around like that."

"I did this time! I know that I did. This feels more than right," She jumped up and down with excitement, "I can feel it! The magic just feels right this time." Aunt Mira secured the pot over the spout and poured the potion into a skinny glass vial. The potion she created had an iridescent purple color that seemed to shine when the glass enveloped it. Then I watched her scribble onto the label a quick title, even going so far as to draw a heart to go with it like she did with most of the love potions that she had made. That way they would be able to be found again once she put them up on the shelf. When they didn't work to break the curse, she would cross it out and give it a new title reflecting whatever purpose they served and move on.

"Are you going to give it to someone?" I inquired, as I had often been curious about Mira's potions and her willingness to try so hard for something that seemed impossible.

I know that we all feel it, even if it is just a little part of us. It was the longing when we see a couple who had been together for over 50 years, the ones who still hold hands walking down the street and who have a look of love struck in their eyes. The old couples who discuss their children with strangers in the lines at the grocery store because they are so proud of them. There was a very small chance that I would ever take a sip of any of the potions Aunt Mira made. It didn't matter how much I wanted to understand love or at least the idea of love, there was no way that I could put my faith into something with so much uncertainty.

The door swung open, the bell above sending off a ring as the first customer of the day came in. I took that opportunity to send myself back behind the counter before the young girl had a chance to see me standing beside Aunt Mira signaling that I was ready to do any sales.

It was dangerous to use our magic in front of people, but sometimes the temptation was too hard to handle when it felt so second nature to us all, especially to those like Aunt Mira who used their magic as often as they could. Thankfully most of the time the person who was supposed to be watching would just assume that they hadn't really seen what they thought they had. Humans wanted to believe in normal, which is why they typically ignored the things that should catch their eye.

"Welcome to the Corner Shop. What can I help you find today?" Aunt Mira chimed out with her welcoming smile. I felt a burst of magic in the room as the vial Aunt Mira was holding in her hand landed securely in the pocket of the apron I was wearing.

I think her name was Ninnie, but most people had just talked about her family as a whole, not choosing to single any of them out. Many of the people in our city had started calling them a silly name that had been made up when we were in elementary school. The townspeople called them the Weird Walkers, as all her family sat in the back row of the church, never attended public school, and only went into the town monthly. Their house was found on the very edge of the city, near the woods where few would be willing to venture out of fear of the things that were held there.

There was something to be said about keeping to oneself and their family. A family like mine was often together, excluding those who were different. Many of the people in town tried to stay away after they started feeling that something was strange about us. Grandmother always said that it was nothing about us, rather the other people, that they often had a sixth sense about things like us. That helped them stay safe, just as they were weary of a tiger or bear, knowing that even at their most tame, they were still dangerous. That advice hadn't really made me feel any better when I was a teenager, wondering why no one took me to prom or let me be a part of their social group. This girl, Ninnie, did not seem like she was a part of that crowd. She had not a single part of her that was nervous to approach either one of us, but she was nervous about something else — evidenced by the way her eyes bounced from object to object within our store.

I sent out a little magic, using a spell Grandmother had taught me last week. It helps us to know the intentions of someone's actions before they approach, looking to gain perception from the situation. It was helpful when I managed to get it to work for me, but my magic was uncertain of her intentions because it came back to me without a purpose to expose. Because of this, I made sure to stay within their circle to be able to hear their conversation just in case Aunt Mira needed anything.

The young girl seemed as though she was getting ready to say something several times, she opened her mouth to then close it quickly. I watched the nervous way she wrung her hands together and how her eyebrows pinched together in distress, bringing out some wrinkle that showed years of intense thinking and worry despite her young age.

"What is it that you are looking for? I could make a few suggestions of our items on sale or show you things we have on display?" Aunt Mira asked her softly, gesturing around the room. She grabbed a straw basket and went to give it to her; I could tell that she was also growing tired with anticipation as well. "With our fall line out now, there are plenty of autumn inspired smells to go around. We just updated our displays this weekend so even if you have been in before, it is a completely new store, and we are both more than happy to point some things out for you if you are looking for something specific today."

Ninnie took a deep breath, pulling her confidence together before continuing to speak to us. "I know you are a witch."